T

"Robin has done it again! ... e taking this

"Get ready for a wild ride through the back streets of Oxford and London's busy underground. *Sisterchicks Go Brit!* is a joy to read and a delightful reminder that it's never too late in life to take a risk. You'll be cheering as these women dare to follow their hearts and be inspired to revive the dreams lying dormant in your own heart. Thanks, Robin, for treating us to another Sisterchicks adventure full of friendship, faith, and fun."

—MELANIE DOBSON, author of *Going for Broke* and
The Black Cloister

"My only complaint about Robin's latest is that now I want to hop a plane to England! But combine a cup of Earl Grey tea and this charming story, and you're halfway there. Another delightful tale about women helping women to live their lives to the fullest."

—MELODY CARLSON, author of *These Boots Weren't
Made for Walking* and *A Mile in My Flip-Flops*

"Funny, touching, and true to life, *Sisterchicks Do the Hula!* will have you doing the hula (and loving it!) by the last page. Grab your grass skirt, girlfriend—this is one trip you don't want to miss! Robin Jones Gunn is the perfect tour guide for this joy-filled

Hawaiian adventure. You'll feel the sand between your toes, taste sweet pineapple juice, see amazing rainbows—all without having to put on a bathing suit! Your travel partners, two turning-forty chicks, will feel like old friends the minute you hit the beach."

—LIZ CURTIS HIGGS, best-selling author of *Bookends, Mixed Signals,* and *Grace in Thine Eyes*

"*Sisterchicks in Gondolas!* is a true delight. The characters shine, and evocative language will make any reader want to visit Venice. Biblical truths are portrayed simply yet will touch hearts and lives with their realistic application."

—*Romantic Times* magazine

"If you have a keen sense of adventure, you will love exploring the world with Robin Jones Gunn's Sisterchicks series… The author makes sisterhood and friendship into an incredible treasure, and she uses Scripture in a way to challenge, uplift, and encourage the readers. This is an excellent read."

—BOOK BARGAINS AND PREVIEWS for *Sisterchicks in Gondolas!*

"Robin Jones Gunn makes traversing midlife seem almost welcoming because she has that rare gift of communicating hope amid trial and inner chaos. Robin has found an effective mode of gently lending some instruction to women who sometimes feel overwrought and undone by life's unexpected curves. Women and older teens will relish *Sisterchicks Down Under!* Who says growing older can't be fun if you have a friend to share the journey?"

—FAITHFULREADER.COM

sisters of the heart

best buddies

soul sister

friends forever

kindred spirits

sister-friends

SISTERCHICKS
Go Brit!

girlfriends

pals for life

chum

confidante

gal pals

ally

true blue

Robin Jones Gunn

a sisterchicks® novel

SISTERCHICKS GO BRIT!

MULTNOMAH
BOOKS

SISTERCHICKS GO BRIT!
PUBLISHED BY MULTNOMAH BOOKS
12265 Oracle Boulevard, Suite 200
Colorado Springs, Colorado 80921
A division of Random House Inc.

All Scripture quotations, unless otherwise indicated, are taken from the Holy Bible, New
Living Translation, copyright © 1996. Used by permission of Tyndale House Publishers
Inc., Wheaton, Illinois 60189. All rights reserved. Scripture quotations marked (NIV) are
taken from the Holy Bible, New International Version®. NIV®. Copyright © 1973, 1978,
1984 by International Bible Society. Used by permission of Zondervan Publishing House.
All rights reserved. Other Scripture quotations on pages 283–84 are taken from The Message
by Eugene H. Peterson. Copyright 1993, 1994, 1995, 1996, 2000, 2001, 2002. Used by
permission of NavPress Publishing Group. All rights reserved.

The characters and events in this book are fictional, and any resemblance to actual persons
or events is coincidental.

ISBN: 978-1-59052-755-9

MULTNOMAH is a trademark of Multnomah Books and is registered in the U.S. Patent and
Trademark Office. The colophon is a trademark of Multnomah Books.

SISTERCHICKS is a trademark of Multnomah Books.

Library of Congress Cataloging-in-Publication Data
Gunn, Robin Jones, 1955-
   Sisterchicks go Brit! : a novel / Robin Jones Gunn.
      p. cm.
   ISBN 978-1-59052-755-9
   1. Women travelers—Fiction. 2. Female friendship—Fiction. 3. Americans—Great
Britain—Fiction. I. Title.
PS3557.U4866S5627 2008
813'.54—dc22

                                        2007047056

Printed in the United States of America
2008—First Edition

10 9 8 7 6 5 4 3 2 1

For Julee and Marion
with "Sisterchicks Forever" memories
of our Oxford tour and teatime in Olney

Deep in your hearts you know
*that every promise of the L*ORD *your God*
has come true.
Not a single one has failed!

JOSHUA 23:14

Prologue

Some dreams and wishes, I believe, are of the dormant, time-released variety. They aren't forgotten over many years or through many changes in life. They don't shrink during their hibernation. They simply wait to come true when the dreamer and the wisher need to believe all over again.

Kellie and I definitely needed to believe all over again.

Kellie's dream was to have an interior-design business.

My wish was to go to England. Ever since I was fifteen, I had wished I could stand on Westminster Bridge in London and gaze up into the golden face of Big Ben. Silly, I know. But that was my wish.

Never did either of us imagine that Kellie's dream would overlap my wish when we were both fifty-four years old. We were, by our own unspoken rules, past the point in life at which one should venture out in a new direction.

But that was before we met Opal.

A bright-eyed, seventy-nine-year-old pixie of a woman, Opal slipped her silken hand into mine on the doorstep of her English cottage and said, "Elizabeth, my dear, do you know what the dearest kindness is that a woman can offer herself in the autumn of her years?"

I shook my head.

"It is the gift of giving herself permission to take risks."

And then she winked at me.

That's when I understood that sometimes a hibernating dream or a dormant wish must be ushered out of its cavelike sleeping chambers and nudged right up to the cliff's edge of possibility. It must take a deep breath and step off the edge into nothing but untamed air. In that risk-taking moment, the wish just might discover its wings and fly. I've seen it happen.

I never would have known any of this if I hadn't been late to meet Kellie for coffee two years ago. I dashed into Brew-La-La to escape the jellybean-sized drops of warm, Floridian rain.

Right behind me was a petite feather of a woman dressed in a bright green jogging set. She was shielded from the drops by a spotted gray umbrella, making her look like an overgrown mushroom.

I held the door for her and located Kellie across the café, ensconced in one of the cranberry red chairs in our usual corner. She waved to me with a beckoning "over here" sort of hand motion. The walking mushroom responded by striding across the room and planting herself in the cranberry red chair intended for me.

In that moment my dormant wish was nudged toward the mouth of its cave, only I didn't know it. Kellie's dream was about to be ushered right to the cliff's edge of reason, but she had no clue what was coming.

All I did was hold open the door. All Kellie did was wave. Everything else happened at a blink-of-an-eye speed after that.

Several months ago Kellie and I were retelling our story to one of Kellie's clients. As usual, we started with the encounter at Brew-La-La. Kellie described the winsome way Opal walked through the open door and made herself at home in the middle of our lives.

Kellie's client said, "She sounds like your fairy godmother in disguise."

"Disguised as a mushroom," I said and quickly added the description of Opal's green "stem" and toadstool-colored umbrella.

I also said that while we didn't consider Opal to be fairy godmother material, she did qualify for the British sort of fairy. "In English literature fairies are known for their mischievous antics. What Opal did right before our eyes was as quintessentially pixie as you can get."

Then Kellie said, "I don't think it was Opal the Fairy Godmother who granted my dream and Liz's wish. I think it was our heavenly Father."

I nodded in agreement.

"He's the One who knows what dreams lie dormant in the cave of every human heart," Kellie added. "He's the One who nudges us forward and invites us to trust Him."

I watched Kellie's client tear up, and I knew my friend was working in her vein of gold. Women invited her into their homes to rearrange their furniture. Before she left, Kellie often rearranged their hearts.

As for my wish, in many ways I'm still living it. My husband, Roger, said, "You always did like getting lost inside a good story." My life does feel like a good story. Only I don't feel lost inside it. I feel at home.

Sometimes I think about how it felt, stepping off the cliff's edge into that untamed air. I remember the sense of being embraced by the everlasting arms of the Maker of all dreams and all wishes. He held both Kellie and me close in that free fall of faith, and it was there, in that closeness, that I could hear His heart more clearly than I had in years.

All of this because of Opal and her reminder that we're never too old to take a risk.

That Opal.

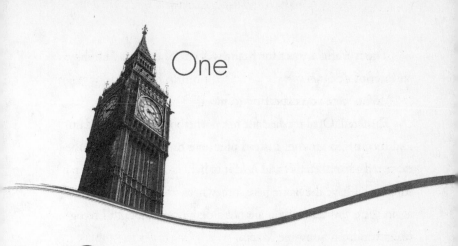

One

On that pivotal day at the Brew-La-La, the first thing I noticed about the tiny, determined woman as she assumed command from the cranberry red chair was her British accent.

"I do appreciate your willingness to meet with me here on rather short notice. I'm Opal. I spoke with you yesterday." She adjusted her trifocals and with an open palm patted the side of her poofed-up white hair.

Kellie gave me a what-is-going-on-here look. All I could do was shrug.

"As I indicated on the phone," Opal continued, "I'm fully prepared to pay your regular fees. My only question is, when might you be able to provide me with an estimate?"

"I'm sorry," Kellie said in a tone that revealed her instinctively smooth and professional demeanor. "I think you might have me confused with someone else."

Opal blinked. "Are you not an interior designer?"

The truthful answer for Kellie was yes. She was, as a hobby, an interior designer.

"Who were you expecting to meet?" I asked.

Flustered, Opal reached for her pocketbook, undid the clasp, and rummaged around. Instead of a note or a business card, she extracted a handkerchief and held it in her left hand as if for moral support. "I have the name here somewhere." She looked at Kellie again. "Are you certain you are not a designer? I thought I recognized you from Sunshine Manor."

Kellie smiled. "My aunt used to live at Sunshine Manor. Did you know Martha Wojckski?"

Opal's expression lifted. "Yes, of course I knew Martha. Her apartment was beautifully decorated. Which is exactly why I'm meeting with a designer. I'm afraid I'll go mad if I don't have a change of color on the walls soon. Do you happen to know who designed your aunt's apartment?"

Kellie blushed. "Actually, I did."

Opal sat up straight. "Then I should like to engage you for the work needed on my apartment."

"I'm not a professional interior designer," Kellie said quickly. She looked to me for backup, but I didn't agree. Kellie had done wonders with my small home, and her home was a masterpiece. She had wanted to pursue designing for well over a decade but had never taken the first step toward that dream. If Opal was going to push Kellie off the cliff by inviting her to take this risk, I wasn't going to stop her.

"You did such a lovely job with your aunt's apartment. If you're available, I would certainly like to hire you."

"What about the other designer you were going to meet here?" Kellie asked.

Opal looked around and glanced at her watch. "I don't think she's coming. We only had a tentative meeting arranged, which is why I was so hopeful when I saw you wave. In her message yesterday she said she was reluctant to take on the project since I live at Sunshine Manor. Apparently there are difficulties in working within the limitations set by the association."

While Opal was talking, I had been giving Kellie all the non-verbals I thought she needed to recognize this as a golden opportunity she had better snatch.

Kellie may have had one eye on my affirming expressions, but she definitely had both ears open to Opal.

"I know," Kellie said to Opal. "They do have some strict rules. I found a way to work around some of the restrictions. They aren't that complicated. We just have to file the necessary forms."

"Does this mean you'll come to give me an estimate?"

Kellie swallowed.

I gave her my most encouraging smile.

"All right," Kellie said with a hesitant sort of nod. "Sure. Why not? When would you like me to come?"

The next afternoon I accompanied Kellie to Opal's apartment. My presence was partly for support and partly because I was fascinated by Opal. Her accent reminded me of Mrs. Roberts, a woman who had been important to me during high school.

Sunshine Manor was all of two blocks from Brew-La-La. We found number 2017 and knocked. Opal opened the door, and I offered one of my best smiles to Kellie's first unofficial client.

I don't have a lot of stunning attributes like Kellie with her gorgeous, thick auburn hair and her warm, perceptive eyes. My hair is flyaway and fair like my skin. But I do know how to smile. I can almost always get others, even pouting children, to smile back when I give them a generous grin.

Opal invited us inside. "May I offer you some tea?"

Kellie and I slid into straight-backed chairs at a round table in the corner. A pudgy, rose-strewn china teapot and a plate of gingersnaps awaited us. We sipped Earl Grey from china teacups balanced on saucers, and I felt like we were little girls playing dress-up. This was a stretch for us. Kellie and I were decaf-grande-triple-nonfat-latte-in-a-to-go-cup kind of women.

I tried out what I hoped was proper British tea-party conversation. "Have you lived here long, Opal?"

"Not long. Sixteen years. My husband lived in Orlando as a child. He was determined to return and spend his final days in the sunshine. He did exactly that. I've been alone the past eight years."

"Where did you live before coming here?" Kellie asked.

"I lived nearly all my life in a small town in England called Olney."

"I always wanted to go to England." I sat up a bit straighter. "Especially London."

"Is that so?"

I nodded with the same eagerness I had felt about England since I was fifteen.

"Do you have plans to visit London soon, then?" Opal asked.

"No, not soon. Someday maybe."

"Maybe sooner than later," Opal said cheerfully. "You'll find London to be a delightful city."

I leaned forward in my best tea-party posture and shared my small secret with Opal. "I've always had a hopeless crush on Big Ben."

Opal studied me as she swallowed a nibble of her gingersnap.

Kellie, of course, knew of my fascination with all things British but particularly the top tourist sights of London. However, when the disclosure of my long-held wish was followed by a pensive silence, she moved the conversation to another topic.

"What sort of decorating ideas did you have in mind for your apartment, Opal?"

Turning her attention to Kellie, Opal said, "I am ready for a complete change. I would like a more cheerful color for these walls. Yellow, I think. One can live within the belly of a pale salmon for only so long."

She unfolded a prepared list and read to us her extensive changes.

Kellie listened thoughtfully. "You have some lovely pieces of furniture. Once the walls are painted, these dark woods will look much different than they do now. I know an excellent upholsterer who could re-cover your wingback chair and give it a new look."

"That would be fine. Just so long as none of the colors is pink. Nothing pink." Opal rose from her chair with surprising agility and reached into her pocketbook. "For what amount should I draft the check?"

"How about if we draw up an agreement first?" Kellie suggested. "It will take me a little time to put together a preliminary proposal. I could return later this week, if you like."

"Lovely. I will expect you on Friday at the same time. Would that suit you both?"

Kellie and I exchanged glances. I wasn't part of the arrangement, but I didn't have a particular reason to bow out at this point.

"Friday would be fine," Kellie answered for both of us.

And that's how our regular teatimes with Opal began.

Kellie poured herself into the transformation of Opal's little nest, and I assisted in small ways. I hit an excellent sale at a fabric store and found the exact material we were after for the cushions on the four straight-backed chairs. I also was able to snag superior quality sheets at an outlet store and a gorgeous pale yellow matelassé bedspread from Portugal.

The entire redecorating process took a little over a month, and the results were stunning. Kellie and I were greeted by name at the front desk whenever we arrived at Sunshine Manor, and Kellie soon had requests for renovations from two other residents.

We were on our way to pay our final official visit to Opal when Kellie pulled into the parking area and said, "You know what I like about doing all this for Opal? I like helping someone who can't drive around town or pick up a paintbrush and make these changes on her own. It was the same way with my aunt. If this is the last home she'll have, she needs it to be lovely."

"I agree. And you know what I've loved about this past month? I've loved watching your creative side run free. I think it's time for you to get a business license."

Kellie's soft brown eyes always gave away her secrets long before her lips agreed to participate in any sort of confession. "I think so too. I even have a name for the business."

"Really? Let's hear it."

"K & L Interiors." She watched my reaction closely as we walked toward the entrance of Sunshine Manor.

"It's a simple name," I said, doing an on-the-spot evaluation. "It's easy to remember. K is for Kellie, right? And L is for…"

"You."

"Me?" I stopped walking. "Me?"

"Yes, you. Liz, we could do this together just like we did for Opal. No one can hunt and gather like you. The bedspread and sheets you found were perfect. And that table lamp was ideal. We're a team. We've always been great together on projects."

"But this is a business, Kellie."

Her eyebrows raised in an expression that said, "So?"

"I'll think about it," I said, even though I already knew my answer. I didn't want to do anything that could jeopardize our friendship. Kellie and I had thirty-two years of friendship to our credit. However, two of those years had been absolutely terrible. I didn't want to be in that terrible place ever again.

"Just think about it, Liz, okay? I talked to Martin, and he thinks it's great. His actual words were 'It's about time.' Will you talk to Roger and see what he thinks?"

I nodded. My affable husband probably would say it was a good idea. But I knew I wouldn't join Kellie's endeavor.

We took the elevator up to Opal's floor and stood by her front door with a gift basket brimming with new tea towels and a tin of loose-leaf Earl Grey to replace all of Opal's tea we had drunk during the past few weeks.

Opal let us in with a Mary Poppins sort of efficiency and invited us to have a seat on her reupholstered sofa. She thanked us for the gift basket and then proceeded to hand an envelope to each of us.

"Go ahead and open them." Opal grinned in her innocent-as-a-lamb way.

This was awkward. I shouldn't be paid for any of the work. It was Kellie's gig. "I can't accept this." I slid the unopened envelope back across the coffee table. "Thank you, though, for considering me."

"How can you say you can't accept it when you don't even know what's inside?" Opal was on her feet, rosy faced with excitement. "Open it. Please."

Kellie and I opened the envelopes in unison. Inside we found airline tickets to what I always had considered the most romantic-sounding airport name in the Western world: Heathrow.

I was holding a ticket to my childhood wish in my hands. Too stunned to cry, I gleamed. That's what Kellie said later. She said my face was so red and radiant I was shooting gleam-beams all over the room.

Kellie immediately began the string of questions. All the answers from Opal started with yes. Yes, this was for real. Yes, Opal was sure she wanted to do this. Yes, she remembered my saying on our first visit that I had always wanted to go to England. Yes, the tickets were booked for next Monday. And, yes, she knew that we had current passports because she had slipped that question into a conversation two weeks ago.

I calmed down, but my smile stayed at full sail. Opal poured the tea. Kellie sat in sweet, stunned silence. Both of us had just put the china teacups to our lips when Opal pulled out her final surprise of the day.

"We are going to have such a lovely time."

Two

"We?" I echoed, slowly lowering my teacup and looking Opal in the eye. "Did you say *we* are going to have a lovely time?"

Opal didn't miss a blink. "Yes, I'm going with you. Did I not mention that fact? My sister, Rose, is immensely eager to meet you both."

Kellie placed her teacup and saucer on the end table. "What exactly did you have in mind for this trip, Opal?"

"I plan to stay in Olney with my sister, of course. I'm sure the two of you will have lots of sights you'll want to see."

Apparently the relief in our expressions was evident because Opal dipped her chin in her childlike way and asked, "Oh, me. Did you suppose I was inviting myself along for the tour?"

Kellie and I offered slight nods.

Opal chuckled. "I've thought about this so much that I forget you haven't been privy to all the details in my little head.

I do confess I was so overcome with the thought of surprising you that I didn't fully consider how my presentation might appear."

"That's okay," I said quickly. "We just want to be clear on the expectations."

Opal's only request was that we assist her to and from the airport and get her safely to her sister's home in Olney. Kellie and I felt confident we could accommodate her request, so we accepted the generous invitation enthusiastically.

That afternoon Kellie and I made hotel arrangements for London. Kellie's husband, Martin, worked for one of the large resorts in Orlando and constantly was accumulating free nights at partner hotels. Since Opal had contacted him a week and a half earlier with her happy idea, Martin already had pulled together a list of London hotels that would honor the discount available to his family members. That first step was easy. We booked a honey of a hotel on Oxford Street and clicked on every photo the Web site provided. We would be sleeping like royalty in fourposter beds with puffy down comforters and lounging about in complimentary robes and slippers.

Even though five days is a ridiculously short time to prepare for such a trip, Kellie and I worked like crazy to get everything in place for our big jump across the pond. We are a good team when it comes to focusing on a project.

I went into what Kellie called my "hunt and gather" mode, and for the next two days I kept our computer at home humming as it printed out a ream of sightseeing information from a variety of helpful Web sites.

Roger looked at my research. "Are you going to have enough time to do all this?"

My lighthearted answer was, "If not, we'll just have to go back."

He smiled. "Maybe I'll go with you next time."

I appreciate my husband. He's solid, affirming, and strong. His weak spot is that he only likes to try things after someone else has tested the waters, so to speak.

Several years ago Roger's company sent us on a cruise to the Bahamas. It was the first time either of us had been out of the country and is the reason I have a current passport. At every buffet on the ship, Roger waited until I sampled the food before trying it himself. It took him three days before he was acclimated and relaxed enough to enjoy the final day and a half at sea.

I was glad I was going into this uncharted British territory with Kellie. If I ever did return to England with Roger, it would be a much easier trip once he knew I already had tried the underground system and tested a few restaurants.

This position of being the first to take the risk felt more empowering than I would have imagined. My husband called me "a brave woman," and I liked that he thought of me that way after thirty-one years of our sedate life together.

The only detail Roger said he was concerned about was the agreed-upon responsibility of driving Miss Opal to her sister's house. I showed him on a map that the town of Olney was located in Buckinghamshire north of London and estimated to be an hour-and-twenty-minute drive from the airport.

"You're planning to rent a car?"

I nodded.

"Which one of you wants to drive on the opposite side of the road?"

My empowerment high wobbled and waned with his question. Not to be daunted by the challenge, I set up an appointment with a travel agent for the next morning. Kellie met me there.

The travel agent put us at ease, saying she had been to England many times and had rented a car on her last visit. "Renting a car is certainly an option, but you'll find the train and bus systems to be easy and efficient. In many cases public transportation is much less expensive than gas and parking."

"What about taxis?" Kellie asked.

"Taxis are readily available. They can be expensive, but they're just as much a part of the London experience as the double-decker buses and the underground. You should have no trouble getting around."

The travel agent provided us with helpful maps and brochures. We left her office feeling more confident about how all this was going to work. Our plan was that after getting Opal to her sister's, Kellie and I would head right back to London on the bus and check into our luxury hotel. We might even catch a play later that night if everything ran smoothly. The list of options was long.

With a round of hearty blessings from our husbands, extended limits on our credit cards—just in case—and our passports tucked in thin fabric pouches hung around our necks, we headed for the Orlando airport on February 23. I couldn't stop smiling. My childhood wish was about to come true.

"I would prefer the center seat," Opal said sweetly as we boarded the red-eye flight to Heathrow. "I have heard the window seat can be drafty, and I don't care for the aisle seat because of all the movement and bumping about."

"I'll take the aisle," Kellie said. "I had three sons, so I got used to a lot of movement and bumping about a long time ago."

I gladly took the window seat, excited out of my skin over the possibility of having a first peek at England's grassy hillsides as we approached our destination.

Before the plane had left the runway, Opal was asleep. Her middle position made it impossible for Kellie and me to do what we had planned during the flight. We were going to put our heads together and look through all the info I had compiled on what to see in England.

"Why don't I look over the information now?" Kellie suggested once we were in the air. "We still have the bus ride to Olney when we can go over details together."

I handed over the prized binder to her. She plugged in her earphones and contentedly listened to in-flight music while going over the tome of options. The front section had a list of all the theater performances scheduled during our time in London. Many of the theaters offered their unsold seats through discount ticket booths in Leicester Square, which wasn't far from our hotel. I loved the idea of starting off with a play our first night in London and hoped Kellie agreed.

One thing we had decided was that we would let the days come at their own pace. We would see all we wanted to see, when we wanted to see it, without turning into sightseeing maniacs. At least that's the way Kellie had worded it two days before we left. I told her I couldn't guarantee that I wouldn't embarrass her at some point with my enthusiasm. She said that was fine as long as we made sure we stopped every day at four for what she already was calling "a proper spot of tea."

I had no problem agreeing to that. Opal had gotten us into a very enjoyable little habit with her four o'clock teatimes.

"Something for you to drink?" the flight attendant asked as her cart blocked the aisle.

I almost said "tea" since her timing coincided so perfectly with my thoughts. But then I remembered from my travel research how extra vitamin C helps fight jet lag. I had also read it is best to avoid caffeine until you have time to adjust to the sleep rhythm in a new time zone.

"Orange juice," I said, feeling like a savvy traveler, even though this was my first trip across the Atlantic. The tea would wait.

"Something to drink for your mother?"

"Oh, she's not my...she's..." Opal was sleeping and didn't rouse even though I was talking over her. "I think she's fine for now."

"Do you know if she would like the chicken or the pasta when we serve the meal?" the flight attendant asked.

I looked at Kellie, who had removed the earphones and tuned in to what I was saying to the flight attendant. Neither of us had any idea what Opal's preferences were in food or in anything else, for that matter. We had spent weeks with her, and yet we knew very little about her. She liked her newly painted yellow walls and her new ceiling fan. And she liked gingersnaps with her tea. Aside from that we were both at a loss.

"Chicken?" I guessed.

Kellie nodded. It was a fairly logical choice. Who didn't like chicken?

Apparently Opal didn't.

She woke a short time later when the enticing fragrance of hot food reached our aisle. I noticed she ate the roll, the salad without dressing, the green beans, and all five of the miniature white potatoes. Her chicken went untouched.

"You must not be a big fan of chicken," the flight attendant commented as she cleared Opal's tray.

"Never have cared much for the foul fowl." Opal's soft smile and little play on words managed to evoke a chuckle from the previously somber flight attendant.

"Did you get enough to eat?" the attendant asked.

"Yes, thank you."

"Opal," I said, waiting for her to turn my direction before making my small confession. "I was the one who ordered the chicken for you. I didn't know what you liked. Are you sure you got enough to eat?"

"I'm quite content, really. If I know my Rose, she will have tea ready for us. We should be arriving at just about teatime."

"Tell me about your sister," I said.

"There's not much to tell, really. Rose lost her William a year ago. She lives in the same house we grew up in. Olney is a lovely town. It was a lace-making village, you know. All the best lace for the British royalty came from Olney." Opal covered her mouth as a kitten-sized yawn escaped.

"We should probably nap while we can." I nodded at Kellie, who had already given in to the drowsiness that followed the meal. Opal closed her eyes and seemed to drift off immediately.

I flexed and unflexed my cold toes. Opal was right about the draft next to the window. It was chilly. I closed my eyes and tried to think warm thoughts. I didn't sleep, but resting in sync with the airplane motor's hum was nice.

Several hours later the tip of my cold nose touched the airplane window as we made our descent. All I could see below was what looked like a batch of peach and white cotton balls. We continued to descend through the clouds, then clouds, then more clouds, and then suddenly there was a break. All I saw was the approaching black strip of the runway. Our arrival was in a London fog, but we were here! And I was about to set foot on English soil.

Three

Opal kept up just fine as we followed the lines through to customs at Heathrow Airport. She had a U.S. passport, apparently because of her husband's dual citizenship, and calmly pulled it from her purse.

Kellie and I had to do an odd sort of twisting and tugging to release our passport pouches from their safe hiding places under our shirts. A woman behind me in line said, "Trust me, you'll draw more attention to yourself as a tourist with those pouches than if you keep your passports in a safe place in your purse. Just make sure your purse is close to your body at all times. You'll be fine."

"Thanks." I gave her a quick glance. She looked streamlined with her shoulder bag and walking shoes. She must travel a lot.

The corridors we had to walk through after customs were long. I wished I had worn more comfortable shoes. Kellie and I offered to locate a wheelchair for Opal if she was growing weary.

She turned down the offer and kept on truckin' right beside us all the way to baggage claim.

Our suitcases arrived, and we loaded them onto what the sign referred to as a "trolley" instead of a "cart." That's when I realized how challenging this part of the trip would have been for petite Opal to manage by herself. While the charming little imp had creatively bamboozled us into escorting her on this journey, clearly she would have had difficulty navigating it on her own. I felt a funny sort of admiration for clever Opal as well as a gathering sympathy for the limitations that come with aging.

We hung close together as we exited baggage claim. I had the transportation papers in hand and announced that our next job was to find the train that would take us to Milton Keynes. From there we would take a bus to Olney. If we needed help, I felt comforted knowing we could ask any of the uniformed airport assistants. For such an enormous airport, Heathrow was fairly easy to navigate.

Just as we were moving out into the general meeting area of the terminal, we heard someone call Opal's name.

A tall man who appeared to be about Opal's age waved at us. He wore a heavy, camelhair coat buttoned up to his neck. "Opal! Over here, Opal!"

She stopped short, drew in a wobbly gasp, and in a matter-of-fact tone said, "Oh, me. It's Virgil."

We made our way around to where the beaming man looked

down on stunned little Opal with admiration. His large coat surrounded him like fur on a yak.

"Rose told me you were coming." He continued to beam in an older-gentleman sort of way.

Opal's face glowed right back, even though she seemed to be fighting to remain subdued.

Before Kellie or I could introduce ourselves, we heard a muffled yelp. The wet nose of a white, long-whiskered dog poked out from between the second and third buttons on Virgil's coat.

"All right, then, Boswald. You remember the rules. Stay tight until we get back to the car. You can see the pretty ladies soon enough." He looked at Kellie and me and, offering a polite nod, said, "I'm Virgil, by the way. This is Boswald. You'll be able to meet him proper soon enough."

"I'm Kellie. This is Liz."

"Elizabeth." He lowered his head in a playful bow. "Queen Elizabeth. I'm honored."

"Virgil," Opal said firmly, "why have you come?"

"Why to see the queen, of course," he said with a crooked grin at me. "Your majesty." He bowed his head to me once again.

"I'm afraid you have wasted a trip coming all the way here to collect me," Opal said, still standing her ground. "We have made our arrangements. We are going to take the train."

"So I was told. However, I have come anyway, haven't I? I suppose I could blame the trip on Boswald." Virgil leaned down and spoke into his coat. "You wanted to come see the aeroplanes take off, didn't you, Boswald?"

Kellie and I exchanged glances. I felt as if I had stepped on stage in the middle of an odd performance of *Peter Pan* and here was the uncle who had lost his marbles.

Opal didn't budge. The change in plans seemed to fluster her. Or was it the indomitable character standing in front of us who rattled her world? I had a feeling this wasn't the first time he had done so.

"Well, then," Virgil said with an air of calm confidence, "we had best be on our way. The car is waiting for us in the car park."

The dog yipped again. Virgil patted his coat. "Steady on, Boswald. Not another word from you."

Boswald held his yip, and so did Opal. She straightened her shoulders and walked beside Virgil toward the exit. The two of them made quite a pair. Opal stood no more than four feet ten inches tall. Virgil had to be close to six feet. Off they went, the little Florida orange blossom and the big yak.

Kellie reached for my arm. "Who do you suppose he is?"

"I don't know, but did you see the expression on Opal's face when she spotted him? That was a long-lost-love look for sure."

"Do you think we should go with them?"

"Are you kidding? I wouldn't miss this for anything."

"No, I mean, do you think it's safe to go in a car with him?"

I laughed. "Are you worried about 'stranger danger'? Because I will agree that Virgil is stranger than most."

"Liz, I'm serious. This is so odd. We don't have to go with him."

"But we do need to stay with Opal all the way to Olney. That's what we promised her we'd do."

"Okay, but let's have a backup plan. If we get to the car and either of us feels it's not a safe choice to let Opal go with Virgil, then we agree to kidnap her and take the train."

"Agreed," I said. "Although if we try to run off with Opal, Virgil might let Boswald loose and send him after us."

Kellie lightened up. "If we have to make a run for it, we'll dump the luggage, put Opal on the cart, oh, I mean the trolley, and we'll both push and run as fast as we can."

"All the way to Olney," I said with a laugh.

"All the way to Olney."

We exited the terminal and entered the car park. A sharp, unwelcome blast of cool air met us. I zipped up my jacket and had a feeling my lightweight coat wouldn't be hearty enough against the damp February air. Having lived in Florida all my life, I'd had a hard time imagining this sort of chilliness. I had packed two warm sweaters in my suitcase and could wear both of them under my jacket if necessary.

Kellie was wearing a fleece pullover covered by a knee-length raincoat. The combination seemed to make the chill tolerable for her.

"Here we are." Virgil stopped behind a compact red sedan. "Out you come, Boswald. Say hello to the ladies."

A wide-eyed, whisker-twitching terrier nosed his way out from under Virgil's coat. Boswald checked out Kellie and me with a long string of yips, as if we were doggy biscuits in a shop window.

Virgil opened what he called the "boot" of the car and loaded the luggage. I stepped around to the front passenger's door and asked Opal, before she slipped into the car, if she was comfortable with the situation.

"I'm a bit chilled, if that's what you're asking."

"No, I'm asking if you feel safe riding in the car with this man. Do you trust his driving?"

"Oh, Virgil is quite capable. He made it to the airport, didn't he?" Her expression softened. "Rose, I'm sure, would not agree. But she never had a fondness for Virgil."

"But you do, don't you?"

Opal blinked quickly. Her twinkling eyes looked like two smooth, blue marbles.

I smiled and helped her into the front seat while Kellie assisted Virgil with the luggage. If Virgil had lost some of his marbles, it seemed pretty evident where two of them ended up, all sparkly and blue.

Kellie came around the side and raised her eyebrows as if this was part of the code to determine if we were going to proceed. "Everything okay?"

I nodded, still wearing a snug little smile.

"Oh-kay." Kellie scanned my expression.

"No, really. I think everything is okay."

The two of us clambered into the backseat and sat close, with the smaller pieces of luggage under our feet. I leaned over and whispered in Kellie's ear, "I think we've stepped into an unfinished love story."

Kellie was a big fan of holding secrets when it came to other people's romances. All three of her sons had confided in her the plans for the how, when, and where of their proposals to their girlfriends. She had kept all three secret from everyone but me. I knew none of the details, but in the midst of each of their love stories, I could read enough in Kellie's brown eyes to know what was coming around the corner.

Virgil started the car engine, and Boswald made himself comfortable on the floor next to Opal's feet. She didn't seem to mind the dog being underfoot.

With my elevated longing for romantic impressions, my first views of England from the car window weren't what I expected. My fairy-tale mind had conjured up expectations of an immediate view of Stonehenge, the Tower Bridge, or the moors where Heathcliff roamed throughout Emily Brontë's *Wuthering Heights*.

Instead, the view was of afternoon traffic in a modern city complete with billboards, asphalt, concrete buildings, and tinges of diesel fumes in the air. Aside from the trucks being narrower and shorter than most trucks in the U.S., I hardly could tell I was in another part of the world.

Telling my brain that we weren't actually driving on the wrong side of the road turned into a challenging mental exercise for the first five minutes or so. Virgil kept his full attention on the motorway. Opal watched the road as astutely as a copilot, and Boswald remained curled up at her feet, taking a nice little nap.

The invitation to join his occupation suddenly felt over-whelming. I closed my eyes for only a moment, and I nodded off. Funny how I had such a hard time trying to sleep on the plane while I was anticipating our arrival in England. Now that we were here, I zoned right out.

How we reached Olney without incident, or what the coun-tryside along the way looked like, I can't tell you. I have no idea. When I opened my eyes and squinted at the world around me, Virgil was pulling the car into a narrow gravel driveway that ran alongside a small two-story brick house. The car stopped inches in front of a wooden shed that was topped with a moss-covered, sloping roof. By American standards the shed was far too small to be used as a garage, but that appeared to be the building's function.

"All ashore who's going ashore." Virgil turned off the engine. "That includes you, Captain Boswald."

I stepped out of the car and stomped my feet. Overhead, the midafternoon sky was heavy with clouds hanging low and gray. The air carried the scent of wood smoke. I noticed the sprouting grass along the side of the house. Our Florida grass rarely sports such a crisp, bright shade of green. A few pale lavender crocuses tucked under the blanket of green stretched their brave necks up from the muddy earth. The surroundings weren't of King-Arthur-and-Camelot status, but as I exhaled and saw my breath form a detached cloud, I clearly grasped I wasn't in Orlando anymore.

The two-story cottage in front of me wore its steeped roof like a pointed cap. The house was accented with clean, white-wash trim around the window frames and front entrance. I glanced up and down the narrow lane and noticed that the colors of the houses here were the primal colors of quarried lime-stone and sandstone. The bricks were in soothing shades of terra cotta and fawn instead of the familiar deep red of the bricks often used in the U.S. Dark timber was employed only for accent and structural support.

I started up the walkway, lugging one of Opal's large suitcases, and was the first to arrive at the doorstep. At my feet was a mat that I kept looking at, trying to decide if the words woven into it had the same meaning here as they would have where I came from. Instead of the customary "Welcome," two words appeared in bold, black letters: "Go Away."

Deciding the message was meant in a witty sort of way, I looked over my shoulder and saw Opal coming up the walkway a few feet behind. She took steady steps toward the front door and called out to me, "The door should be open. Rose never locks her doors in the daytime."

Before I could test Opal's theory, the front door opened, and standing before me was, well...Opal.

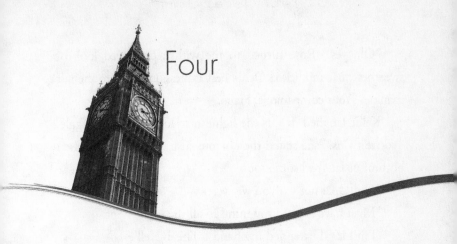

Four

"You're twins!" I exclaimed.

I did a double take of the two sisters and then a triple take. The only visible difference between the dynamic duo appeared to be what they were wearing. Their hairstyles, eyeglass frames, posture, and expressions were identical. I tried to remember how long it had been since Opal said the two of them had seen each other. How extraordinary that they were so alike!

Kellie walked up just as the two sisters exchanged a quick, tender embrace and started talking over each other's sentences.

"I told him not to go to the airport," Rose began. "But since when has he ever listened—"

"It's a wonder he found us."

"You must be—"

"Terribly. Sitting for so long is—"

"I put the teakettle—"

"I told my companions you would."

"Oh, yes." Rose turned to me with a clear-eyed look of sweetness that mimicked Opal's best expression down to the last twinkle. "Your companions. Hallo."

Kellie laughed. It was the lightest, friendliest sort of giggle. "You're twins!" she stated the obvious just as I had done. Then both of us laughed some more.

"Did Opal not tell you we were—"

"Must have slipped my mind in all the excitement."

"I'm Liz." I extended my hand. "This is Kellie."

"Queen Elizabeth." Virgil came up behind us with Opal's suitcase.

Rose ignored him. She grasped just my fingers in a dainty, ladylike handshake and repeated the gesture with Kellie. "Do come in. You must be—"

"Chilled to the bone, I should say," Opal answered for us, stepping over the threshold.

"Do you need help with the rest of the luggage, Virgil?" Kellie asked.

"Oh, yes. Of course," Rose answered for him, waving us on our way back to the car. Virgil was already halfway there.

The sisters went inside and closed the door. Kellie and I were left standing on the Go Away mat.

Kellie laughed, and I was right there with her.

"Twins!" Kellie said as we headed back to the car. "Have you ever seen two such identical twins? I thought I was seeing double. Is that one of the effects of jet lag?"

"I have no idea. But I will tell you this whole day is starting to feel like something out of *Alice in Wonderland*. I think you and I have tumbled down a peculiar sort of rabbit hole."

We stopped at the back of the car. Before reaching for the last of the luggage, Kellie and I both looked around as if we had shared the same thought at the same moment.

"Where's Virgil?" we said in unison.

Kellie laughed again. "Now look who's acting like twins!"

Neither Virgil nor Boswald was anywhere to be seen. Kellie checked the front seat of the car. "The keys aren't in the ignition. Maybe he took Boswald for a walk."

I lowered my voice and leaned close. "Maybe he felt slighted by Opal's response to his gallant effort to greet her at the airport and went straight home with Boswald."

"Or to the nearest pub," Kellie whispered.

We giggled again. "I'm starting to think jet lag brings on an insatiable desire to laugh a lot."

"I think you're right, Liz. Let's lug these suitcases into the house before we're too chilled. It's cold out here."

I almost made it to the front door before feeling the urge to laugh again. This time the desire was brought on by the silly doormat.

Kellie seemed to have missed it and asked as she stepped inside, "What do you think? Should we leave the luggage here in the entry?"

To our left was a narrow flight of hardwood stairs. We could hear Opal's and Rose's muffled voices finishing each other's sentences from a room around the corner.

"Opal?" Kellie called softly.

"We're back here, in the breakfast room."

"Where would you like us to put your luggage?"

I whispered, "Please, oh please don't say upstairs."

"Leave them right where you are for the time being, and—"

"Come join us," Rose concluded.

Kellie and I stepped around the corner of the small entry and entered a sitting room. A small sofa and a leather chair flanked a dark wood coffee table with stacks of books and a potted violet on it. The window that looked out on the street had an inlaid section of stained glass in a triangular pattern of yellows, blues, and greens. Even with the dense clouds overhead, the light through the stained glass offered the sitting room a magical touch.

A hobbit-sized hearth occupied the center of the far wall and was canopied by a mantel that appeared to have acorns and leaves intricately carved into the wood.

"Oh, Lizzie, look at the rug." Kellie's face expressed admiration. "Morris-inspired, I'm sure of it. It's gorgeous."

The rectangular rug was a blend of greens and blues with a repeating pattern of beige accented by touches of red tones. It was pretty. Pretty old and faded, but it had a pleasing pattern.

Kellie bent down to touch the threads and took a closer look at the rug. "Wow, this is really something. It looks old enough to be inspired by the original."

"Original what?"

"The original William Morris pattern Strawberry Thief. It was one of his most successful designs."

I took a closer look and realized the repeating beige in the pattern was actually well-defined birds, and the red touches were strawberries. Interlaced around them were vines and flowers in rounded shapes. Even though the rug was faded, the design seemed dimensional.

"It is gorgeous," I said.

"Morris was a genius. He coaxed Britain to move away from those eighteenth-century heavy velvets and ornate chairs and bring the simple beauty of the outdoors into the home. I know I've talked about him before. He's one of the Pre-Raphaelites who launched the Arts and Crafts movement more than 150 years ago."

My expression must have conveyed how impressed I was and at the same time how lost I was. Kellie's hobby was reading up on decorators and collecting books on their various styles. If she had mentioned this British designer to me, I didn't remember him.

"William Morris was the one who said, 'Have nothing in your houses that you do not know to be useful or believe to be beautiful.'"

"Oh, okay. Sure. I've heard you quote that before. I love that quote."

"Well." Kellie made a sweeping gesture toward the rug. "Useful and beautiful."

"And apparently enduring if he made this rug 150 years ago."

"His firm might have made this rug," Kellie said. "Or a rug maker who used his designs. But Morris couldn't have made this exact rug. If he had, it would be in a museum."

I had no idea this man was so famous. It made me wish I had hunted and gathered some information on Morris before we left. I would love to see Kellie's face if she could view some of his original work in one of the many museums in London.

"Have you lost your way?" Opal called out.

"We're in here!" Rose added. "Keep coming."

I reached for the handle on the closed door at the end of the small sitting room. On the other side of the door, Opal and Rose were seated at a round table in a square room painted sunshine yellow with white trim. It was easy to see now where Opal's inspiration for the colors in her apartment had come from. High windows in the breakfast room brought in light that seemed to suit the large fern in the corner just fine.

"Close the door behind—" Rose said.

"To keep the heat in," Opal finished. "Tea?"

"No, thank you," I answered for both of us. "We need to be on our way to the hotel."

Rose and Opal looked surprised. "But it's nearly four," Rose said. "I have some sandwiches prepared. Nothing fancy—"

"Minced ham is fancy enough," Opal added.

"Yes, of course. Minced ham. Opal's favorite. And the scones are nearly ready from the oven."

Kellie looked as if the chance to pause for tea was a great idea. I reminded myself about our agreement to let the days come at their own pace and to stop for a proper spot of tea.

I smiled and took the seat offered to me. London and my beloved Big Ben would still be there two hours from now. We could see a play tomorrow night or the next night or both nights if we wanted. Kellie and I were being invited to "take tea" in a cozy cottage in an English village with two engaging women. Why wouldn't we stay for such an opportunity?

As Kellie lowered herself into the chair next to Opal, I also lowered my expectations of what Kellie and I needed to accomplish that day. When Charles Dickens lived in this fine country he wrote about "great expectations." I was preparing to write the first chapter of Kellie's and my British story and entitle it "Realistic, Reduced, Willing-to-Get-Sidetracked, Yet Nonetheless Delightful Expectations."

With that adjustment in place, I found it much easier to agree with Kellie when she commented on the beautiful tablecloth. It was a quality linen fabric with a pattern in bright blues and yellows. The teakettle was an electric one with a fat cord attached to the wall by a large, round plug. The teacups waiting for us were in the Spode blue Italian pattern, the same china Opal used to serve us at her apartment in Florida. I no longer felt a little silly, as if we were sitting down to a little-girl tea party. I felt very grown-up and honored to be at this table.

Kellie began the conversation by commenting on the rug as well as other design features she admired in Rose's charming cottage.

Rose seemed impressed with Kellie's familiarity with Morris and the Arts and Crafts movement. She said the rug had been in the family for as long as they could remember. Opal said it had always been a favorite of hers too.

"Do either of you know of a museum where we might see some of Morris's designs?" I asked.

Rose and Opal spoke at once, overlapping each other.

"Kelmscott Manor, of course," Rose said. "Although I don't know if they offer tours every day, and it's not in London."

"Neither is the Red House," Opal added.

"Well, the V and A, of course," Rose concluded.

Opal nodded and sipped her tea.

"And that's a museum?" The name wasn't ringing a bell. The British Museum showed up in all the lists of recommended tourist sights, as did the Tate Britain Gallery, Madame Tussauds Museum of Waxworks, and, of course, the National Portrait Gallery. I hated asking what the V and A was, but after all, I was a tourist. I still had my passport in a pouch tucked under my clothing to prove it.

"Why, the Victoria and Albert," Rose said.

I made a note and decided I would gather more information from our hotel concierge on the subject.

Within the first five minutes of sitting at Rose's table in that warm and cheery breakfast room, I felt my feet thaw, along with the rest of me. The tea served was more than just a beverage; it was a defroster. An elixir that brought me into the present.

I lifted the china teacup to my lips, and my smile curled around the smooth rim. For a decaf-grande-triple-nonfat-latte-in-a-to-go-cup sort of woman, I was curiously finding myself being won over to the wonder of tea. Or perhaps it was the ceremony of sitting down and "taking tea." Here we were, on the other side of the world, yet it didn't seem unusual or out of place for the four of us women to be together like this, sipping tea and chatting. Was this elemental camaraderie true of women the world over? Around such a table, how could we not be of one heart?

Rose pushed away from the table with some difficulty and exited through a swinging door that led, I assumed, into the kitchen. I leaned toward Opal and said, "What happened to Virgil?"

"No one seems to know. He's been that way ever since his wife passed on some years ago."

"No, I mean, where did he go?"

"Oh. Home, no doubt. He'll be back. He always comes back."

Five

Rose returned to the sunroom just then with a plate of the warm scones. "You really must try these with some of the lemon curd." She pointed to a small bowl, which contained pale yellow jam.

Kellie and I both tried the lemon curd and said, "Delicious!" at the same time. We gave each other "twin" looks and tried not to tumble into a fit of laughter.

Rose seemed pleased with our assessment and settled back into polite conversation, discussing our flight and the traffic we'd encountered leaving Heathrow.

The thin sunlight through the high windows was waning. In the twilight that now hushed the breakfast room, the pull of slumber became overpowering. I wondered if Kellie was feeling the same draw. A short nap sounded so good right then.

When the teapot was emptied, Kellie glanced at me, and I knew it was time for us to be on our way.

Just as Tolkien had invented an elfin language in his Lord of the Rings novels, Kellie and I had developed an entire code of facial movements. Over the years we found we could communicate with each other when no one else knew what our pursed lips or tilted head meant.

I gave Kellie a "yes, let's get going" dip of the chin and tried to think of how to insert the "we must be on our way" line into the conversation. I started with, "Would you like us to carry your luggage to your room, Opal?"

"She's staying downstairs with me," Rose said. "The guest room upstairs is ready for the two of you."

"Oh, we're not staying," I said. "Did Opal not tell you? We're going on to London this evening. We have hotel reservations."

Rose shook her head with clear disapproval. "Hotels are so expensive, don't you think? I was just reading in the paper the other day that London is one of the most expensive cities in the world for hotel accommodations. Hong Kong was on the list as well. Can you imagine that?"

"We have a very good, discounted rate," Kellie said. "My husband is employed by a major hotel chain."

"Nevertheless, you might want to reconsider staying here with us."

"If only for this first night," Opal added. "You must be weary."

Of course we were weary. But we had a lot of plans for the week, and none of them included lingering in Olney.

"You certainly won't be able to see much of London by the time you get there this evening," Rose said.

I knew I was too tired to be responsible for any decisions at that point. Kellie looked like she was succumbing to Rose's and Opal's mesmerizing words as well.

"You've gone to all the trouble of bringing in your bags already," Opal said.

"And you've come on such a long journey..."

Kellie and I gave each other a look that said, "Well?"

"I suppose we could call the hotel and cancel for one night." Kellie glanced around the room for a clock. "I have to call before six o'clock, and we would be leaving here first thing in the morning."

"I'll bring the phone to you." Rose pushed away from the table and got up stiffly.

The reservation adjustment took only a few minutes. The next order of business was to move the suitcases to the bedrooms. I already was dreaming about stretching out on a bed with the covers pulled up to my chin. Oh, the thought of being luxuriously reclined and toasty warm!

As Rose cleared the table, I followed Opal and Kellie back through the sitting room to the entryway and found the suitcases right where we had left them. We wrestled Opal's luggage down to Rose's room at the end of the hall.

Kellie stopped in front of the closed bedroom door while Opal turned the knob and entered cautiously. "Oh, me," she said under her breath.

Kellie and I turned to each other and made our "yikes!" faces.

Everything in the room was pink with lots and lots of roses. The wallpaper, bedspread, curtains, and even the cloth lampshades on the two end tables beside the double bed were plastered with large, pink roses. Four framed paintings of pink roses covered the wall above the dresser. I had never seen anything so pink and so rose strewn.

Just then Rose joined us. "What do you think, Opal? You haven't seen my room since the renovation."

"It suits you well."

"Yes, I think it does. Now, shall we show our guests their room?"

The upstairs room was simple and sparse without a single rose to be found. This had been Rose and Opal's childhood bedroom. The lace-doily-covered dresser still displayed a few of their small trinkets, including a music box in the shape of a Swiss chalet and a yellowed baby's hairbrush accompanied by a nearly toothless comb.

The narrow twin beds sloped in the middle but were sturdy enough for us. The angled roof rose above a padded window seat where one square window with thick glass provided the only view of the outside world. It was a distorted view of neighboring cottages interspersed with an occasional modern home.

"Do you think it's a good idea that we stayed?" Kellie asked after the twins left us to settle in.

"I don't know. I think so."

"It's kind of quaint, isn't it?"

"Very quaint. This room is how I always pictured the Darling children's nursery."

"What nursery?"

"In *Peter Pan.* Did you ever read the book?"

"No. Liz, you keep popping out with all these literature comparisons."

"British literature," I corrected her.

"I love it. I didn't know you had so much British literature stored away in your memory. When did you read all those books?"

"In high school."

"The only novel I remember reading in high school was *The Great Gatsby.* Oh, and *The Grapes of Wrath,* I think." Kellie pulled her cosmetic bag out of her suitcase and looked up at me. "Why did you read so much British literature in high school?"

I smiled at the memory before giving Kellie information I had never told her. "I had a tutor when I was fifteen."

"You did?"

"Her name was Mrs. Roberts, and she had a fabulous British accent."

"Why did you have a tutor?"

I sat on the edge of the sloping twin bed. "I was very sick, and I thought I was going to die."

Kellie chuckled.

I didn't.

She raised her eyebrows. "Lizzie, you're serious. What happened?"

I realized that when you've been the closest of friends for decades, it's natural to think you know everything about the other person. Kellie knew my brothers by name. She knew what size shoe I wore before my two daughters were born and what size I wore now. She knew that I had a cat in first grade called Inky Boo and that my eyelids swell whenever I inadvertently eat salsa laced with jalapeños. But Kellie didn't know this story tucked deep in my history.

"My sophomore year of high school I had to stay in bed from October to February, and my parents hired a tutor."

"What illness did you have?"

"Mononucleosis."

"You had mono?" She grinned. "Who did you kiss?"

I cringed as if I were fifteen again and answered with the same indignation I had back then. "No one."

"I'm just kidding." Kellie obviously had caught the edge in my voice.

"That's what everyone said."

It really wasn't my intention to come across so strong or indignant to Kellie. She had no way of knowing that this ancient history still carried a sting. My reputation throughout high school had been tainted by rumors that I had "gone too far" with some guy over the summer and that's how I got the kissing disease.

"I didn't kiss anyone," I said more calmly. "I got strep throat, and it developed into mononucleosis. The mono went after my liver, and I developed jaundice. By the second month of the illness I tested positive for hepatitis."

"Oh, Lizzie, you *were* sick."

"My skin turned a nauseating shade of yellow, and so did the whites of my eyes. It was awful. I really thought I was going to die. Then Mrs. Roberts came with her basket of books. All the British classic novels. She read to me for hours, and after she left, I kept reading."

"That's why you and your girls are such great readers. You passed that love of literature on to them."

"It wasn't just the literature I loved. Mrs. Roberts also brought travel brochures of England. She said they were our geography lessons. I would open those glossy, accordion-folded brochures, and she would tell me all about the sights in each picture. I memorized the pictures: the Tower of London, Westminster Abbey, Buckingham Palace, St. Paul's Cathedral, Trafalgar Square, and, of course, the red phone booths."

"I can't believe I never knew this."

"I almost told you a few years ago when you asked why I didn't want to go with you to the blood drive. Do you remember that?"

Kellie nodded. "My nephew was in the hospital. You said you couldn't donate blood. I thought you just meant you couldn't make it to the hospital that day."

"No, I can't donate blood. My medical records show that I had hepatitis, and that means I'm not qualified to be a donor."

Kellie sat on the edge of her twin bed looking at me compassionately. "Your sophomore year was when you made your birthday wish to go to England, wasn't it?"

I nodded. "When my fifteenth birthday came that December, I wished I could go to London one day."

"And then you never got to. Until now."

"This might sound odd, but a trip to England wasn't my real wish back then. I just wanted to be well enough to go to London if the opportunity ever presented itself. I guess my wish was really about getting healthy."

"Then I would say a double wish has come true for you today, sweet friend. You've been healthy enough to come for forty years. And now you're here."

"I know." My face warmed as a childlike sense of delight came over me. "We're here, aren't we? We're in England."

"And tomorrow morning we'll be in London."

However, the next morning we were still in Olney. Like Ben Gunn who was marooned on Treasure Island, it appeared we might never get away from the well-meaning twins. At least I wanted to believe they were well meaning.

Six

The good news about our night at the Olney cottage was that we slept well. The layers of blankets on top of the twin beds in the upstairs dormer were wondrously heavy. They pressed us into deep sleep the way a leaded apron presses a patient into the dentist's chair when x-rays are taken.

Kellie and I stayed in bed as long as we could the next morning, whispering back and forth about our plans for the day. We decided that as soon as we were up and about, we would call a cab to take us to the train station. We would go straight to London, and even if we weren't able to check into our hotel right away, we would leave our luggage there and start taking in the sights.

Kellie was the first to slip out of bed. She tiptoed downstairs to the "loo," as Opal had called the bathroom the night before. It was impossible to wash and flush without the sound of running water echoing throughout the house.

Moments later I could hear Rose and Opal tottering down the hall, each telling the other to keep her voice low but issuing the instructions loud enough to stir the neighbors. I tried to picture the two of them sharing the rose-strewn double bed the night before. My imagination contrived a cartoon image of their round faces smiling, both positioned exactly the same way, with their billowy white hair on the pink pillows, and both of them holding the top fold of the covers with just their fingers showing, like kitten paws.

Kellie slipped back into the room with a grin on her face. "Wait till you see this. They're wearing matching bathrobes and matching hair scarves. I'm not kidding. It's the cutest thing you've ever seen."

"How did they manage to come up with matching robes?"

"Who knows? They certainly seem happy to be together, though. Oh, and Rose said she would have tea for us in the breakfast room 'shortly.' I'm not sure what *shortly* means, but I told her we were almost ready to leave."

"I wish they hadn't gotten up. I didn't want to wake them."

"I know," Kellie said. "But it's impossible to do anything quietly in this house."

We quickly finished getting ready and zipped up our suitcases. Kellie and I entered the breakfast room and discovered that Rose intended to serve us more than just tea. She had prepared soft-boiled eggs, and each of us had one waiting at our place, balanced pertly in a china eggcup. In the center of the table was a small, upright metal rack. In between the rounded wire separators, Rose slid pieces of toasted white bread. She did it with such efficiency it almost looked as if she were "filing" the slices for us, the way file folders are placed alphabetically in a filing cabinet. Jars of marmalade and strawberry preserves were added to the assembly, and the teapot was filled with boiling water from the whistling electric kettle.

Rose sat next to Opal and asked if we would like to join them in saying the morning grace. Kellie and I bowed our heads. In unison Rose and Opal repeated in a lyrical tone,

> *"Come, Lord Jesus, be our guest*
> *and let these gifts to us be blessed.*
> *Amen."*

"Amen," Kellie and I said.

"I trust you both slept well," Rose said as I tried to spread jam on my slice of bread without getting the toasted crumbs all over the table.

"Yes, we did," I said.

Kellie nodded. "Very well. And you?"

"We both slept—"

"Well enough."

"Thank you for your hospitality," Kellie said. "It was very kind of you to let us stay."

"Yes, thank you," I added.

Opal gave a sweet little shake of her head and said something that caught Kellie and me off guard. "You Americans do tend to overstate everything."

That's when we realized the twin we had supposed was Rose that morning was really Opal. Rose was the one who had been sitting beside us at the table all along while Opal was the one serving the eggs, tea, and toast. In their matching robes it was nearly impossible to tell them apart. I kept scrutinizing their hands and faces, trying to find some distinguishing mark.

I spotted the one clue I thought I could count on. On her wedding ring finger, Opal wore a gold band with an inset iridescent stone. An opal. I had first noticed the ring when she was serving us gingersnaps at her apartment a few weeks ago. *Opal wears the opal ring.*

"More tea?"

Before Kellie or I could respond to Rose, Virgil made a grand entrance. And I do mean a grand-slam, crazy-as-a-Mad-Hatter entrance.

He swung open the back door in the kitchen and entered the breakfast room with Boswald tucked under his arm. Boswald was wearing an argyle sweater with a harness-style leash over his midsection. Over Virgil's barreled midsection he wore a matching argyle sweater covered by a striped navy blue and white apron. On his head a tall, floppy white chef's hat skimmed the top of the doorway.

"I'm on my way to commence with the pancakes." His

booming voice seemed to fill every inch of the previously peaceful breakfast room. "Who's coming with me, then? Opal? Miss Kellie? Elizabeth?" He gave me a bow, and his puffy white hat gave a flop as he teased me with "Your majesty."

"You're early." Rose glanced at the clock on the wall. "It's not quite—"

"Eight," Opal finished for her. Neither of them expressed any other surprise or disapproval over Virgil's outfit or performance.

I glanced at Kellie. She had covered her mouth with her hand and seemed to be trying valiantly not to laugh aloud.

Virgil offered no explanation for his outfit or his behavior. He simply stood his ground with his gaze fixed on Opal. She was peering into her teacup.

With a wave of her hand, Rose said, "We'll be over—"

"Soon," Opal said softly.

"Well, I should hope." Virgil gave Kellie and me a nod, causing his Poppin' Fresh chef's hat to slip forward. No matter. He turned without making an adjustment, and we heard the back door close behind him.

I could tell Kellie was having a difficult time holding in her mirth. We sat quietly, anticipating some sort of explanation.

"Honestly, Opal, I don't see why you encourage him so. Virgil will never amount to—"

"He's still Virgil," Opal said with finality in her voice. "I wish you would—"

"Perhaps I shall."

"Lovely."

"Indeed."

With sheltered glances at each other, I pursed my lips, and Kellie pressed a finger to the side of her nose. We just had witnessed the most civilized sibling argument ever. The subject of debate was obviously Virgil, and it appeared Opal had acquired a small victory.

"Shrove Tuesday," Rose said out of the blue.

"Excuse me?" Kellie said.

"Today is Shrove Tuesday, in case you were wondering why we're going to church this morning after the race."

Kellie quickly put down her teacup and covered her mouth as she coughed. I expected tea to come out her nose at any minute. We definitely had walked in on the Mad Hatter's tea party this morning.

"You're welcome to come with us, if you like," Opal said.

"Thank you, but we need to be on our way." Then to prove my determination, I quickly munched my last bite of toast and gave Kellie a let's-get-outta-here-before-the-White-Rabbit-shows-up look.

She didn't catch my message. Instead, she asked a fateful question. "What is Shrove Tuesday?"

Rose stared at her sister as if Opal had invited sheer heathens into her home. "Shrove Tuesday is the day before Ash Wednesday, which is, of course the beginning of—"

"The season of Lent," Opal finished.

"I'm familiar with Lent," Kellie said. "The forty days before Easter. And Ash Wednesday, of course. But I've never heard of Shrove Tuesday."

Opal tilted her head to her sister and in a confiding voice said, "They attend the church I told you about. The one with the *contemporary* service."

Rose lifted her chin and gave a knowing look. We weren't heathens. Just reprobates.

"What does *shrove* mean?" Kellie asked.

I tried to get her attention and subtly pointed at my watch so she would realize we needed to be on our way. But she was caught up in the discussion.

"The Shriveners were the priests in the Middle Ages," Rose said. "They listened to confessions and prepared contrite hearts for Lent. Hence, *Shrove* Tuesday, the day when the faithful abstained from such rich foods as eggs, butter, and milk—"

"To demonstrate a penitent heart."

Rose wasn't about to be outdone by her sister, so she added, "Which is why the women used up those ingredients on Shrove Tuesday before the church bells called the repentant to gather—"

"At midday," Opal concluded, as if everything should now be clear to us.

It wasn't.

Kellie asked, "Is Shrove Tuesday the same as Mardi Gras?"

"The French!" Rose and Opal crossed their arms in unison.

"How disappointing that the Americans are familiar with the French Mardi Gras but not with our Shrove Tuesday." Rose shook her head at Opal, as if her sister were responsible for our lack of understanding.

"Doesn't Mardi Gras mean 'Fat Tuesday'?" Kellie asked.

"Yes. Not *repentant* Tuesday or *confession* Tuesday," Rose pointed out with an air of disgust. "They turned it into a day of debauchery."

"But the idea is the same, isn't it?" Kellie asked. "The premise is to feast on Tuesday and start forty days of depriving yourself on Wednesday."

"Well…" Rose tilted her head from one side to the other, as if weighing the question. "Yes and no."

"They don't know about the race," Opal said in an aside to Rose. It sounded like another apology for us.

"Does the race have anything to do with women carrying frying pans?" Kellie asked.

Now I thought I was the only sane guest left at this tea party. Kellie had gone bonkers right along with Virgil and his pancake hat.

"I saw the sign on our way into town. Liz, didn't you see the sign with the women in head scarves running with frying pans?"

"No, I missed that."

"The sign was for the Shrove Tuesday pancake race," Opal said matter-of-factly.

"The race is today," Rose added.

"So," Kellie said slowly putting together all the clues, "does that mean Virgil was going to make pancakes?"

"Of course."

"What did you think?" Opal asked with her endearing, soft-eyed innocence.

Neither Kellie nor I answered that one.

"As I said, you're welcome to come if you like." Opal stole a glance at the clock. "We really should get ready to go."

Rose and Opal excused themselves from the breakfast table and left Kellie and me to try to make sense of the last half hour.

"What do you think?" Kellie asked.

"I think it's better for our longstanding friendship if I don't say what I'm truly thinking right now."

"Well, I'll tell you what I think. I think we should go to the race."

I gave Kellie my best you've-got-to-be-kidding-me look.

"It seems like an extraordinary opportunity."

"I'll agree with your choice of the word *extraordinary*. Doesn't all this seem just a little odd to you?"

"What do you mean? We're in an old English village, and we have a chance to observe a very old tradition."

"What tradition? Pancakes? Races? Church on Tuesday? I'm so confused."

"I am too, but I'm strangely intrigued by all this. What do you think, Liz? Could we follow the twins to the race and then come back and get our things and leave right after that?"

"Okay."

"Really? You're okay with this?"

I sighed and gave a resigned shrug. "I can't explain it, but I have the feeling we're being hoodwinked somehow."

Kellie laughed. "What exactly do you think these two little elves are going to do with us? We can leave anytime we want."

"Anytime we want. I'm going to hold you to those words."

"Fine."

"Okay. Fine."

And off we went to the upstairs guest room to get ready to watch some sort of race that involved women in head scarves with frying pans. Never in all my imaginings did I see *this* as the ideal way to spend my precious few days in England.

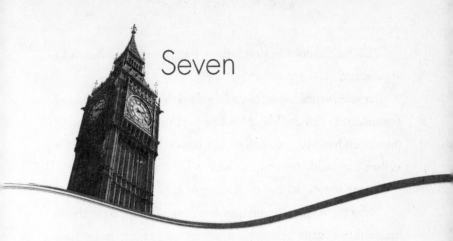

Seven

My theory of being conned by these two sisters wasn't going to carry any weight with Kellie until I had evidence of wrongdoing. So far all we had experienced was gracious hospitality and free plane tickets. Not exactly reasons to accuse anyone of deceptive behavior. Still, the unfolding of these events felt peculiar.

When it was time to go, Kellie and I joined the twins at the front door. My bad attitude and skepticism had dissipated, and I had to smile when I saw their outfits.

Opal and Rose had shed their matching bathrobes and donned matching green knit sweaters and plaid wool skirts. Rose said the new ensemble was her welcome home gift for her sister. The only part of their outfits that didn't match was their shoes. Opal was wearing hot pink tennis shoes, or "trainers," as she called them. Rose appeared jealous of the racy little cuties as she stood next to her sister in her well-worn brown loafers.

"It's a ridiculous notion," Rose was saying as Kellie and I approached.

"It may be ridiculous, but when will I again have the chance? I've made my choice." Opal held a frying pan in which a single, misshapen pancake was cooling. She brushed past us and made a beeline for the kitchen.

"Is everything all right?" Kellie asked.

"Her life in Florida certainly has changed her." Rose shook her head. "My sister has not been quite this bold since the last time she was in the race."

"Opal was in this Shrove Tuesday race?" Kellie asked.

"We both were. Three years in a row."

"Four," Opal corrected her. She had returned to the entry-way wearing an apron and was donning a head scarf. Apparently she was now decked out in the official racing apparel for the Shrove Tuesday pancake race.

"Did either of you win?" Kellie asked.

"No, Isobel Dix won all three years," Rose reported.

"Four," Opal said. "It was four years."

"No, Isobel won three years in a row. Florence won that first year, don't you remember?"

"What year was that?" Kellie asked.

"Nineteen fifty," Opal spouted quickly.

"Nineteen fifty," Rose echoed. At last they agreed on something.

Next to the front door were two lightweight folding chairs.

The twins looked at the stools, then sedately looked at Kellie and me as if they didn't dare ask the obvious. We didn't make them ask. We picked up the stools and followed them out the door.

"I hate to ask another question," I said as we strolled a few feet behind the twins in what felt like proper ladies-in-waiting formation. "But can one of you tell me what this race is all about? I don't understand the connection between the frying pans and the church and—"

"It's a tradition that goes back to the Middle Ages," Rose began. "It started when a churchgoing woman in Olney had not finished making her Shrove Tuesday pancakes. The church bells began to ring a few minutes before midday, calling her to the service. She—"

"Didn't want to leave the last of her butter, eggs, and flour in the pan to burn, so she ran to the church, flipping the pancake in her frying pan. And when she arrived—"

"This part is hearsay," Rose said with a disapproving wag of her head.

"The woman was given a kiss of brotherly love from the vicar in recognition of her noble efforts," Opal finished for Rose.

"And that is why Olney continues to celebrate the pancake race every Shrove Tuesday. Resident women run from the market square to the church at noon."

"Five minutes before twelve o'clock," Opal corrected her. "That's when the church bells are rung."

"And you're going to run in the race this year, Opal?" I asked.

With her shoulders back she said, "I intend to give it a noble effort, like a true daughter of Olney."

I thought I heard a snicker escape from Rose, but I couldn't be sure because the narrow streets were teeming with spectators talking, walking, and reserving viewing spots at the starting line.

As soon as we entered the congested area, Rose and Opal caused an exhilarating stir. The twins glowed, grinned, and all but kissed every baby they saw along the way. Their stature seemed to grow with every greeting. Many of the older residents expressed delight at seeing Opal again. Others—most likely those who were new to Olney—were stunned to see that Rose had a twin and kept doing the same sort of double take Kellie and I had done the day before.

Everyone made note that Opal was dressed for the race and all but hoisted her onto their shoulders by the time she reached the starting line. She was hailed as the wild-card, last-minute entry, but the judges wouldn't go for it.

"The rules clearly state that the race is open only to current residents of Olney. In that you are no longer a resident, Opal, we cannot allow you to compete. Should your residency change in the future, you would, of course, be welcome." The man delivering the news to a disappointed gathering of Opal fans was growing red in the face, which soon matched his red blazer.

Kellie and I went from maids-in-waiting to personal bodyguards as we moved away from the starting line and tried to keep up with a smug Rose accompanied by a humbled Opal.

We rounded the corner of the main street and were directed to Rose's preferred viewing spot. If we leaned forward and looked left, we could see the starting line. To our right, the racecourse wove around a bend before hitting the straightaway to the church. We could see the looming church spire behind the buildings. The location was ideal for viewing the race's start as well as for the reigning princesses properly holding court.

Kellie and I set up the chairs on the front row exactly as Rose directed. My conspiracy theory seemed to be playing out. These two ever-clever twins had taken us on as their handmaidens.

Kellie seemed oblivious to the oddities going on. She was caught up in the village charm and chatted with those seated around us.

"Are you by chance from Liberal?" one of the British bystanders asked Kellie and me.

"Excuse me?"

"Liberal, Kansas. Are you from Liberal?"

"No, we're from Florida."

"I thought you might be from Liberal. They're our sister city, you know. We've been competing with them since the 1950s for the fastest time."

"Are you saying a race like this one takes place in Kansas?" Kellie asked.

"Indeed. The pressure is on us this year. We need a win."

Kellie turned to me. "Maybe next year we should go to Kansas on Shrove Tuesday."

When I saw her merry expression, I realized I needed to lighten up. We were in England. And this was by far the most hilarious and quirky thing I had ever seen. Why was I so uptight?

Opal was seated with her feet tapping in her hot pink sneakers. She held the frying pan in her lap as if ready to jump in the game on a moment's notice. Looking at her made me realize that was the way I needed to position myself for the rest of the trip. Expectant. Flexible.

So what if we hadn't gone to London last night as planned? Why should that ruin my attitude or make me cynical? I took a deep breath of the chilly, damp air and felt my heart mellow.

We watched as a dozen or so racers lined up at the starting point. I hadn't expected such a mix of sizes, shapes, and ages. All the women wore skirts covered by aprons in a wide variety of colors and styles. All of them wore some sort of kerchief or scarf on their heads. And all of them wore modern-style running shoes. It was quite an eclectic array, as each held out her frying pan and listened to the instructions being given by an official-looking gentleman in a red blazer.

"It appears that the outfits haven't changed much since the two of you raced in the fifties," Kellie said.

"Except for the shoes," I added.

Rose gave an uncomplimentary snort.

On the mark of some sort of signal we couldn't hear, the line of women flipped their pancakes in the air just once. It seemed they had to prove their pancakes weren't glued to the pans. The test run of the flying flapjacks brought an eager round of approval from the hundreds of spectators.

"Just about ready," the man behind us said.

The ancient Shrove bell rang out from the church steeple, and off they went! The herd of seriously competitive women with their aprons and scarves hit the asphalt. Images of the past and present raced past us as flapjacks flipped, head scarves flapped, and the women pounded their way toward the parish church of St. Peter and St. Paul.

That quickly, they rounded the corner and were out of view. All except for one lone trotter: Opal.

While we were watching the official race zoom past us, Opal had sprung from her seat and now was trotting along, playfully flipping her pancake. No one was going to tell her she couldn't participate in the race fifty-some years after her last competition.

She flipped her pancake again with an exaggerated grin or grimace. It was difficult to tell which. Both her hands then grasped the frying pan and clasped it right under her bosom. I assumed the wrists-under-the-bustline position was for added athletic support. She wasn't exactly an athlete, but she definitely could use the support.

A spectator behind us said, "The poor dear looks as if she's been harpooned with a long-handled frying pan and is trying to pull it out!"

Rose seemed to share the woman's opinion. She watched her frivolous twin with her arms crossed, shaking her head in disapproval.

Regardless of how Rose or the other woman viewed the unofficial straggler, Opal was the darling of the crowd. As she scuttled around the bend at her one-foot-in-front-of-the-other trotting speed, Kellie and I joined the rest of the crowd to cheer her on. Many of the viewers waved. Some of them, including Kellie and me, laughed joyously at the determination Opal demonstrated.

Then it was over. Opal was out of view. Rose stood, and Kellie and I folded up the chairs. As Rose muttered, we followed the dispersing crowd that was making its way to the church. The disadvantage of being positioned in the middle of the raceway was that we didn't see any of the women cross the finish line, nor did we see the final pancake flip or the scandalous "kiss of peace" from the vicar.

But we did see Virgil when we arrived in the churchyard.

And we saw Opal.

He was beaming. She was glowing. People were taking her picture as she stood beside Virgil in his floppy chef's hat.

"What has happened to my sister?" Rose wasn't looking at either Kellie or me, but the tone in her voice made it sound as if she was charging us personally for the untaming of her twin. "She has not behaved like this since…"

The end of her sentence went unfinished. I wanted to finish it. The ending was right on the tip of my tongue, but I held back from saying it.

Since the last time she was in love, right?

Kellie pulled me aside. "What do you think? Should we leave now?"

"Now?" I surprised myself with my sudden resistance to leaving Olney.

"I'm thinking if we stay for the church service and the pancake feed afterward, we'll be here all day."

"You're right. Yes, we should slip out now. Let's tell the twins."

Kellie and I ushered Rose over to where Opal was posing for the last of her publicity shots. She still was flushed from her admirable trot to the churchyard. We drew her aside and explained to both of them that we needed to be on our way. Their disappointment was blatant.

"We did hope you would stay for the pancakes at least."

"And the church service," Rose said.

I'm sure she was convinced Kellie and I were the undoing of her sister and all three of us incorrigible women from the U.S. were in dire need of a good sermon.

"We'll take the chairs back to the house," I said.

"No need," Opal said. "Virgil can take them for us. He's taking the frying pan back for me."

"The house is open," Rose said. "I don't lock my door during the daytime."

"Well, thank you both so much for everything. We really appreciate your hospitality. Kellie and I will come back here next week as planned."

"We will be here," Opal said. "And do remember that in case you tire of London sooner than you expect and would like to come back early—"

"The guest room will be waiting." Rose stood next to her sister as the two of them fell into their overlapping pattern of talking.

"We have your phone number with us, and we'll contact you if our plans change," I said.

"Have a lovely time in London."

"Thank you," Kellie and I said in unison.

The two sisters stood to the side of the pancake tent and waved at us as we turned to go. I glanced over my shoulder with one last smile. With the sunlight coming through the churchyard, the sisters reminded me of two fuzzy-haired characters in my younger daughter's favorite movie, *The Princess Bride*. Without knowing it, Rose and Opal were mimicking the scene in which the elderly couple stand at the front door of their woodland cottage waving and calling out, "Have fun storming the castle!"

"Do you think we're doing the right thing?" Kellie asked when we were out of the crush of people.

"Definitely. If we stay…"

"I know. We'll never—"

"Get out of here. You're right."

There was a short pause, and then I said, "Did you just finish my sentence?"

Kellie looked at me. "Did I? I thought you finished my sentence."

"I think I did."

"I probably did too."

"Then it's definitely time for us to take our leave of the twins."

We linked arms and tried Opal's trot-walk on the now-deserted streets of Olney, all the way to Rose's cottage.

Eight

We had no trouble arranging for a cab to pick us up at Rose's cottage and to take us to the bus station in Milton Keynes. We did have difficulty once we arrived.

I asked which bus we should take to Oxford Street in London, and the driver as well as the attendant on duty kept asking which coach we wanted. Asking for a coach gave me a mental picture of a Cinderella-style, horse-drawn carriage.

The station attendant said he couldn't understand our accents. We were having a difficult time understanding his accent as well. He seemed amused to see two American women with luggage trying to make themselves understood at a coach station that was primarily used by those who lived in the area.

"We need to go to this hotel." I pulled out my super-overachiever notebook and pointed to a brochure of the hotel where we had reservations. "It's on Oxford Street."

"Oxford." The attendant nodded, understanding at last. He walked us over to a bus that had its engine running and was about to leave. We bought our tickets directly from the coach's driver. He stowed our luggage in the bus's underbelly while Kellie and I joined a small number of travelers who were leaving Milton Keynes at two thirty Tuesday afternoon.

The comfortable seats and steady rumble of the bus jogged Kellie and me into a jet-lag snooze for the next hour. With the steaming sound of the air compression brakes on the coach, we pulled into a narrow lane at a bus station where several other buses were lined up. Kellie and I were both yawning as we stepped down from the bus and waited for our luggage. We then walked away as if we knew what we were doing.

"So." I looked around the moderately small station. "Should we ask someone how to get a taxi to take us to our hotel?"

"Good idea. Although if we go to the other side of this building, we might be able to hail a cab. You would think plenty of them would be hanging out at a bus station."

I followed Kellie and thought how quiet the surroundings seemed for such a large city. Not that I had any idea what part of London we had landed in or how far we had to go to our hotel. I guess I expected more traffic noise. The age of the surrounding buildings and the relative lack of commotion and congestion almost made it seem as if we were back in Olney. I had expected London to be industrial and noisy like it was when we left Heathrow Airport.

"There's a cab." Kellie picked up her pace and raised a hand to flag the taxi driver. He was parked along the side of a cobblestone road.

"Are you free?" Kellie asked.

With a wry grin the driver said, "No, mum, I charge full price like the rest of 'em."

"I meant, is your taxi available?"

"Of course."

We climbed into the back with our luggage, and he started the digital meter. "Where to?"

Kellie said the name of the hotel, and he looked stumped.

"I have it written down," she said. Unfortunately, the reservation papers were folded up in the pouch around her neck along with her passport. She had to do some tugging and wiggling to retrieve the papers. While she did her backseat cha-cha, the meter was running.

Kellie handed the reservation to the driver through the open window between the front and back seats. "The address is there at the top. Oxford Street."

The driver let out a low whistle. "This is going to cost you, mum."

"All right," Kellie said cautiously.

"Are you sure this is where you want to go?"

"Yes. Why is it going to cost so much?"

"This address is in London, mum."

"Yes," Kellie said plainly.

"We're in Oxford, mum."

Kellie leaned back slowly. She didn't look at me.

I asked the most illogical question ever. "Are you sure this is Oxford?"

"Pretty sure, mum. I was born and raised here. But I have been known to make a mistake or two along the way. At least that's what the wife tells me."

Kellie covered her face with both her hands. "I can't believe this."

"We must have gotten on the wrong bus," I said. "We were trying to tell that guy at the station that we wanted Oxford Street, London, and he put us on the bus to Oxford."

"Obviously," Kellie muttered. Her happy-camper attitude had flown south.

"Where did you get on?" the cabby asked.

"Milton-something," I said.

"Right. Well, you have several choices, then. You can go back to the station behind us and ask a stationmaster to make sure to get you on the right coach back to London. The express coach will take you to Heathrow. From there you can take the tube into the city. Straightforward enough. Unless your tube stop is off the Piccadilly Line. You'll be jostling your luggage down a lot of stairs if you're on the Piccadilly. In that case you would be better off taking the train into Paddington. From there you can take the tube or a cab to your hotel."

He was speaking understandable English, but he might as

well have been speaking Martian to us. At that moment his directions were too overwhelming to process.

"Any other options?" I asked.

"You can always stay in Oxford for a day or two." He grinned. "It's not a bad place. Or, if you really like, I can drive you to your London hotel, but I'll have to tell my wife I won't be home for supper."

"What do you think we should we do now?" I asked Kellie.

"I don't know."

It seemed Kellie and I were taking turns having bad attitudes. Mine had dissipated during the pancake race. Kellie's was in full bloom. I had made decisions for both of us many times in the past, just as she had made decisions for us as well. But I preferred not to do so at the moment. Staying last night at Rose's was a mutual choice and had worked out fine. Staying in Oxford would work out better if Kellie and I agreed to do so.

"Have you made up your minds, then?" the driver asked.

"We could stay here," I suggested.

"That means I'll have to call the hotel in London again and cancel before six o'clock. I hate doing that."

"Well, we can go back into the station and take the express coach. I'm fine with whatever."

The driver stretched his hand through the separating window. He held out his cell phone. "Would you like to use my mobile?"

"No, thanks. That's okay." Kellie reached for the door handle. "We can find a phone booth."

The driver kept his hand extended with the phone. His cocky grin didn't leave his face. "I'm sure it's not my place to mention this, but if the two of you weren't able to find the right coach to London, what might your odds be of finding a phone booth this evening?"

He was right, and it was funny. But neither of us was ready to laugh about it. Not right then.

Kellie reached for his phone. Her cancellation call took only a few minutes.

I asked the driver, "What hotel do you recommend here in Oxford?"

"I have just the one. I'll take you there directly." He pulled into the traffic, and we inched our way down a street that obviously was designed centuries before the first automobile puttered through Oxford. The stone walls and brick buildings were as charming, if not more so, than the simple cottages in Olney.

"Oxford seems much older than I expected." I tried to steer the mood away from the gloom that had settled on Kellie.

"That we are, mum. We're a college town, you know. Sixty colleges."

"Sixty?"

"That's right. Students have come here for hundreds of years. Have you heard of the poet Byron?"

"Yes, of course."

"He called Oxford the town with the 'dreaming spires.' Many greats—poets, authors, statesmen, England's finest—have called Oxford home at one time or another in their noteworthy lives. You might find you'll want to stay longer than a day or two."

"I've read a lot of books by British authors," I told the driver.

"Have you a favorite?"

"C. S. Lewis," I said. "The Narnia tales are wonderful, of course, but I think my favorites are the space trilogy. *Perelandra* is my all-time favorite."

"Ah! Then you've come to the right town, and you've found the right cabby. I can drive you past Magdalen College where Lewis taught." The way he pronounced the word *Magdalen,* it sounded like Mawd-lynn.

"Is the college far from here?" I asked.

"Not at all. Would you like me to take you?" He put on the turn signal.

"No," Kellie answered for both of us. "I think we should go to the hotel first."

"Right, then." He kept driving and caught my gaze in his rearview mirror. "You've heard of the Inklings, now haven't you?"

"Yes." I knew that was the name of a writers' group Lewis and Tolkien belonged to for many years. This, however, didn't seem like the best time to show off my interest in Lewis lore since Kellie was in a gulley.

Secretly, I was pretty excited about ending up in Oxford. I hoped I could talk Kellie into some touring in the morning before going to London.

I couldn't believe I now was willing to delay our arrival in London, but here we were, right in the middle of Oxford. Many of my favorite British authors had lived here.

Our driver was explaining a bit about the Inklings—bits I already knew—but then he added, "They met at the Eagle and Child Pub, in the Rabbit Room. You can have a look at the pub whenever you like. Of course, the Rabbit Room sounds more in keeping with the literary themes of the other Lewis."

"Lewis Carroll?" I ventured. "*Alice in Wonderland*? The White Rabbit?"

The driver grinned. "You do know your British literature, don't you?"

"I read a lot when I was younger."

"Do you know his real name?" the driver asked.

"Who? Lewis Carroll? No, I don't."

"Ah! So I can teach you something. It was Charles Lutwidge Dodgson. He taught mathematics right here at Christ Church. He passed on just about the time C. S. Lewis was born."

"What about Tolkien?" I asked. "Didn't he live here in Oxford too?"

"That he did. He was a professor at Exeter."

"Was he really?" Now Kellie was leaning forward. "When my youngest son was growing up, he was crazy about Tolkien's books. He didn't like to read until I bought him a copy of *The Hobbit*. After that, he read like crazy. Is it possible to see where Tolkien lived or taught? I'd love to take some pictures."

"We have a few hours of daylight left. I could take you on that unofficial tour I mentioned, if you like."

Kellie looked at me with a chin-dip nod. I was glad to see her popping back. She was a quicker pouter than I.

"What is the cost of the tour?" I asked.

"We can work out a suitable arrangement."

"We need an estimate," Kellie said.

"That depends. Will you be wanting to see the Kilns as well?"

Neither of us was sure what he was asking.

"I can see by my question that you're not professional pilgrims of all the Lewis sites. If you were, you would be asking for the Kilns, which is the home where Jack and his brother, Warnie, lived. To make it worth your time, I would advise a stop by the Holy Trinity Church and the churchyard in Headington where the two of them are buried."

"Okay," I said. "How much will you charge us for all that?"

"I would say right around fifty pounds."

Neither of us had the exchange rate figured out, so in a way it didn't matter what he said. We wouldn't know what the equivalent was in dollars unless we had a calculator handy.

"Let's do it," I said to Kellie. "Why not? When are we going to be here again?"

"You're right." To the cab driver she said, "We'll take the tour."

The driver put on his blinker and gazed at us in his rearview mirror. "All right then. Tell me this: are you like the couple I had a week ago from California who saw a film and thought they were experts on Jack?"

"Who is Jack?" Kellie asked, more to me than to our driver.

He gave a low whistle. "There's my answer right there. We'll take it back to the top for the two of you."

Switching into a tour guide–sounding voice, our driver said, "Clive Staples Lewis went by the name Jack with his friends because he liked the name, clean and simple. He married an American by the name of Joy Davidman when he was fifty-eight years old. She already had two sons. Jack and his brother, Warnie, adopted the boys after Joy died of cancer. I can take you by the hospital if you like. Or I can even take you to the crematorium where Joy was—"

"No," Kellie and I said in unison.

"Just the Eagle and Child Pub, where you said he met with Tolkien, his house, and the church," Kellie said.

"Got it. The Bird and Babe and perhaps the Kilns."

"I thought you said it was the Eagle and Child?" Kellie asked.

"The Bird and Babe is what those of us who have a familiarity with the Eagle and Child call it. Do you see? Makes sense, doesn't it? Right. Now, where was I? Oh, yes. You wanted to see Tolkien's home as well."

"Yes." Kellie seemed to warm up to the plan and leaned back in the comfortable, wide seat. She pulled her camera out of her bag, and I did the same, ready to take aim and shoot from the vehicle on our Oxford literary safari.

First stop was at the front of the unassuming, whitewashed pub. Our driver snapped a picture of us standing under the round, hanging blue sign that said "The Eagle and Child." The pub sign had the image of an eagle flying in stork fashion, toting a red-headed child wrapped up in a delivery sling and suspended from the eagle's claw.

"Have a look inside at the Rabbit Room. It's in the back to the left. You can't miss it."

An afternoon gathering of customers was tucked in the corners of the compact pub. Our driver was right about it not being difficult to find the Rabbit Room. It was directly in the back of the pub. A small, black sign hung crookedly over the entrance to the separate back room. In the cab our guide had rattled off facts about Tolkien and Lewis being only two of the regular members of the Inklings who met here to discuss their writing between the 1930s and 1950s. A picture of Lewis hung on the back wall above the dark wood paneling. I couldn't imagine comfortably fitting more than eight people in this room. The Inklings must have been a close-knit group when they met here!

Kellie and I snapped a few pictures and slipped out the front door where our carriage awaited us. Next on the circuit was Tolkien's home. To our surprise the street we drove down was a normal residential street with homes that looked as if they were no more than eighty years old. They were nice homes but not fancy or impressive. I made a comment about the ordinariness of the neighborhood, and our driver reminded me that Tolkien received an average college professor's wage until he retired in 1959. He passed away in 1973.

"The room you will see above the garage was Tolkien's study. The Lord of the Rings trilogy was published while he lived in this house with his wife and four children. He had to move, though, due to a rash of hobbit fans who kept showing up on his doorstep."

"I wonder how he would feel about the success of The Lord of the Rings if he were still alive," Kellie said.

Before we could enter into a discussion of the topic, we were in front of the house on Sandfield Road. Our driver didn't park the car in front of the house, even though a wide space was available beside the curb. Instead, he double-parked two doors down. "If you would like to take a quick hop out and stand under the sign over the garage, it makes for a good photo."

Kellie and I scooted up the road and followed his instructions while he sat in the cab with the engine idling. We took turns striking poses next to a trash can in front of the garage. Our conduct on such an unpretentious street in front of such an ordinary garage would have seemed ridiculous if it weren't for the sign affixed to the front of the garage. The commemorative inscription stated, "J. R. R. Tolkien lived here 1953–1968."

"On we go," the driver called to us.

I started for the street, feeling awkward about having just taken pictures in the driveway of what was a private residence. What did the people who lived here think of our trespassing on their property?

"Lizzie, look." Kellie paused by the small front yard. The space was more like an overgrown garden with several trees and ivy climbing up the trunk of the largest one. "Lawn gnomes. Do you see them?"

Kellie was right. Tucked in and under the spreading greenery were several antique-looking lawn gnomes. The chipped paint on their once-red hats and fixed grins made it clear these camouflaged fellows were victims of time and the elements.

Kellie snapped a picture of the garden and the concealed gnomes. Just then we heard a window opening upstairs. Our driver called out, "Come along!"

Hurrying to the cab and sliding into the backseat, I felt the same sort of stealthy rush I had as a teenager when my girlfriends and I would go out at night and string toilet paper in the trees in front of the homes of guys we liked. Then we would run off before getting caught.

"I can't believe we're doing this." Kellie's cheeks looked as rosy as mine felt after the dash.

"I know. None of the tour books promote this sort of snap-and-dash tour."

"There's a reason for that." The cabby caught my eye in the rearview mirror. "None of them is under a court order to keep a twenty-meter radius away from the place of interest."

Kellie and I laughed uproariously at his joke. Off we drove past Magdalen College.

All the way the cab driver kept glancing at us in the mirror.

Nine

"Where to next?" Kellie asked.

"We're off to the Kilns now." The taxi driver ran down a list of dates and facts about Lewis and his brother, Warnie, and how the two of them had bought the house in 1930 and lived there more than thirty years. He went on to explain how the acreage around the Kilns had been undeveloped when Lewis lived there. "If you can be nimble about it, a nature trail at the end of the road will lead you out to a small lake."

My blood still was pumping from all the dashing around at Tolkien's former residence. This was a fun way to see a lot in a short space of time. I was up for sprinting down a nature trail to see a lake. How much more Narnian could this adventure become?

Turning the cab down a private road and into a residential area with several newer homes, our driver slowed down. He spoke rapidly. "You can just about see the Kilns there now, can't you? Brick house on the right side."

Instead of continuing down the lane to Lewis's home, our driver abruptly turned the cab around. In the spin of a moment, I noticed another car parked across the street from the brick house. Someone in the front seat was taking a picture. Not a picture of Lewis's home but of us, of the taxi.

Checking his rearview mirror, our driver said, "I've decided it will be faster if I take you to the church first." He picked up speed and made a sharp turn.

I looked out the back window. The other car was following us.

"Are you sure it will be faster to come back to Lewis's home?" Kellie asked. "We were right there."

"The church is not far. Just across the way from a pub that Jack and Warnie patronized. They walked to church each Sunday and always sat in the same pew. Try the church door. If it's open, you'll find the Lewis brothers' bench on the left side halfway back. It's marked with a plaque. The grave site might be a bit more challenging to find. It's toward the rear area of the cemetery. Do you think five minutes will be enough time, or would you like ten?"

We weren't sure, so he went on to give us specific directions on how we were to turn to the right slightly when we exited the church and how many paces we were to take toward one of the largest old trees in the churchyard. If we kept our eyes open, we should have no trouble finding the flat grave marker with the Lewis inscription. Both Jack and his brother were buried there.

"Why don't you park the cab and come show us?" Kellie asked. "It seems that would be the most efficient way to find everything."

"We'll pay more if we need to," I offered.

"No, I think this will work just fine for the two of you." He checked his rearview mirror again. "Come out of the churchyard the same way you go in, and I'll be waiting. What do you think? Five minutes going to be enough for you?"

"Sure, I guess," I answered for both of us.

We scooted out and trotted down a dirt path under tall, sheltering trees that lined the walkway to the quaint and simple country chapel. The sandstone block construction gave the steep-roofed building that soft golden tone of so many other buildings we had seen in Oxford.

I tried the latch on the church's wooden plank door, and it opened. Right before entering the dimly lit, musty-smelling chapel, I noticed an elderly gentleman strolling through the graveyard. No one else seemed to be around. The events were beginning to take on the feel of a BBC cozy mystery.

Kellie found the pew on the left side about three-fourths of the way back and next to a pillar. The bronze plate on the back of the pew stated, "Here sat and worshipped Clive Staples Lewis (1898–1963)."

Kellie and I stood in the empty chapel and gazed around us. The pulpit was fronted with a large bronzed eagle. The floor was a pattern of dark and light tiles in a checkerboard pattern. The tiles were worn.

"Look at the hair," Kellie whispered.

"Hair? What hair are you talking about?"

"The hair on the Christ in the stained-glass window at the front. He has yellow hair, blond hair. He's an Anglo-looking Christ."

I smiled. At the front of the church was a single stained-glass window with an image of Christ, the conquering King, seated on a throne. "You know what? That image makes me think of the character Prince Caspian in Lewis's book *The Voyage of the Dawn Treader*. I'm wondering if Lewis—"

"Jack," Kellie corrected me. "Aren't we supposed to call him Jack?"

"I wonder if..." I couldn't do it. I couldn't use such a familiar term. "Lewis. I wonder if Lewis sat here and looked at that stained-glass image of a blond king on a throne and imagined the character of Prince Caspian."

Kellie took a seat in the pew that the bronze plate indicated as the place where Lewis sat. "It's possible."

We took turns sitting in the honored pew, shot pictures, and slipped outside, trying to quietly close the heavy door behind us. Together we counted our paces, marking the distance to the grave under the large tree.

The grave site proved much easier to find than our driver had led us to believe. Again we took some pictures, looked around, and then hurried back to where we had been left off, as if we were on a scavenger hunt.

"Why didn't the driver come with us?" Kellie asked.

"I don't know, but did you see the way he kept looking at us after he said other tour guides aren't under court mandates not to trespass?"

"I thought he was joking," Kellie said.

"I did too. But then right before he took that sharp turn back there by the house, someone in a car parked across the street took pictures of us. Then the same car followed us."

"All the way here?"

"No, I think he lost the car at his second turn."

Kellie's eyes grew wide. She looked over her shoulder. "What's going on? You don't think he's going to leave us here, do you?"

"I hope not. He has our luggage!"

"Okay, keep calm." Kellie spread out both her hands and pressed her palms downward, as if trying to quiet a noisy crowd. "We have no reason to panic. At least not yet."

We came to the end of the walkway where we had been left off. Our cab driver was there waiting.

"Everything okay?" I asked after I was in the backseat and buckled up.

"Right as rain. Did you find the grave?"

"Yes, and the church was open, so we were able to go inside. Are we heading back to the Kilns now?"

"We'll give it a go," he said.

This time no other cars were parked along the side of the street. Even so, our driver parked two houses away and checked his rearview mirror as he gave us directions. We were to walk past the hibernating garden, then through the opening in the hedge, and we would be on the side of the brick house where Lewis's study was located. If we stood on the walkway around the side of the house, we were told we could take photos standing in front of two windows; the farther one was the dining-area window, and the closer window was the one Lewis looked out as he wrote.

"Mind you, none of your photos can be used for any sort of publication."

"Okay."

Springing from the cab as if we had received our clues for the next part of this scavenger hunt, Kellie and I tiptoed through the daffodils that had only begun to wake from their winter's nap and to stretch their leafy greens toward the incubator-like sun. Through the opening in the hedge and down the path, we found the two windows, just as the driver had said.

"Here," Kellie said in a low voice as she handed me her camera. We hadn't seen anyone around, but it still felt as if we were on the sly. "Take two shots. One close up and one far away with as much of the house as you can get in the viewfinder."

I snapped quickly and efficiently. Kellie then traded places with me and snapped the same two angles with my camera. Practically jogging, we hustled back to the cab. Our driver had his window rolled down with the engine running.

"The lake," he called to us. "Did you want to see the lake?"

"Oh! Right! The wildlife preserve trail. Where is it?" I asked.

"Behind you." He pointed to a trailhead at the end of the cul-de-sac.

Kellie and I took off at a fast clip. "This is insane!" Kellie tried to tuck her passport pouch back under her clothes. "Why are we hurrying?"

"It's a race! It's a race!"

"Are we on some new reality TV show, and we don't know it?" Kellie laughed.

"Maybe. That would explain the man in the chase car with the camera. We need frying pans and hot pink tennis shoes if we're going to run down the streets."

At the trailhead was a large sign declaring this as the "C. S. Lewis Reserve." Pictures of several birds appeared on the sign, which neither of us stopped to study. If we did encounter any birds on our escapade, it would only be because they weren't fast enough to flap out of our way.

"Careful, Kellie," I called over my shoulder. "This looks pretty muddy."

The trail wasn't long. We came up short at the tranquil lake and quickly took pictures from what appeared to be a newly built observation deck. The trees that surrounded the lake were tall and spacious, shading the area and making it feel like an enchanted corner of the world.

"What do you think?" I asked Kellie. "If we jumped into the lake, would we find a new, untried portal into Narnia?"

"We'll never know, because we're not going to try. Now, smile so I can take your picture."

I smiled. Switching spots, I took Kellie's photo and looked around once more. "This spot reminds me of a scene from *The Voyage of the Dawn Treader*. One of the boys, Eustace, has turned into a dragon, and he hides out in a lair by a small lake like this."

"Tell me about the dragons later." Kellie picked up the pace. She started to slip in the mud, but I caught her by the arm, and she righted herself.

"That was close."

With another grand effort, the two of us hustled our warm bodies back down the vacant trail and out toward the street. The taxi was still there, which was a fairly significant concern I had every time we left our tour guide. But a car that looked like the one that had followed us was pulling into the cul-de-sac. With a sharp turn, the driver of that car blocked the cab's exit.

I grabbed Kellie by the arm and pulled her back to the side of the trail. "Whoa, what's happening? We better stay back."

From our position behind the dense trees and trailing vines, Kellie and I watched what I took to be a peaceable discussion between the two men. The man who stood by the open window of the taxi appeared to be doing all the talking and pointing. His thumb kept jerking back in the direction of the Kilns.

"Maybe he's a tourist asking directions."

"I don't think so." Kellie leaned farther out of our hiding

spot with an ear turned toward the street. "They're having an argument. It's a controlled, civil, British-style confrontation, but it's definitely an argument."

"Are you sure?"

"Of course I'm sure. Look how the guy is standing beside the cab. That's an authoritative stance."

"Oh, Kellie, this is silly. Why are we the ones hiding? Come on. We need to get to our hotel."

"Okay, but act natural. I think I see a neighbor over there peering out her window."

I laughed. "Nothing about this day, this place, or this whole trip has been within the sphere of natural! Why should we start acting like it now?"

Kellie and I strolled down the road toward the cab acting normal. As we approached, the authoritative-looking man was getting into his car and pulling away.

We climbed into the backseat and said we were ready to go to the hotel now.

Our driver muttered something under his breath and kept on muttering as he zoomed out of the private residential area. "Do you want to know what I think of it all?"

Neither of us particularly wanted to know, but he told us anyway with a nasty string of words. Immediately he looked at us in the rearview mirror. "Pardon my French."

"I speak a little French," I said, "and I'm not sure I recognized a single French word in what you just said."

Our questionable cab driver cracked half a grin. "I'll tell you what. The two of you have vinegar, that's what. You'll both go a long way in this world."

He pulled up in front of a small courtyard that led to a well-lit entrance of an old stone building. It didn't look like a hotel to me. It looked as if we were stepping onto a movie set. All the years of having ready access to Disney World and Universal Studios made it hard to believe we were seeing a true medieval courtyard.

We fumbled with our ten- and twenty-pound notes to come up with the agreed-upon charge for the tour.

Still feeling a little rosy, Kellie and I thanked him and expressed how much we'd enjoyed the whirlwind tour, daring as it had been.

"It felt like we were on Mr. Toad's Wild Ride," I said with sincerity.

When he drove off, I told Kellie, "I don't think he took my reference to *The Wind in the Willows* book as a compliment."

"Think about it," Kellie said. "He was the one driving, so that made him Mr. Toad."

"Oh, I see your point. Maybe I have a little too much 'vinegar' sometimes."

"You're not alone," Kellie said.

As we bumped our suitcases over the cobblestone courtyard, she added, "I hope I'm wrong for thinking this, but, Liz, do you think this could be a trap?"

"What kind of trap?"

"Well, look at this place. Does this seem like a hotel to you?"

I told her my theory on Disney-Universal overload ruining my ability to process the real deal.

We were at the door then. Through the glass both of us could see a front desk, a small lobby, and a rack of sightseeing brochures. The place did, in fact, appear to be a legitimate hotel. The attendant at the desk checked us in efficiently and made a recommendation for dinner at Collin's, a local pub down the street. She said they served the best fish and chips in Oxford.

When she saw our hesitant expressions, she said, "I always forget that visitors from the U.S. view the local pub as being the same as an American bar. Think of it as a café or bistro."

An hour later Kellie and I were seated at an old wooden table in Collin's Pub, munching on fish and chips.

"This is really awful," Kellie said.

I was surprised. I thought the fish and chips were great. I even had taken a hint after viewing other diners around us in the noisy quarters and had used the malt vinegar in the shaker bottle on the table to season the fish. "You don't like yours?"

"Oh the fish is great. I love it."

"Then why did you say it was really awful?"

"Because after eating this true, unpretentious serving of fish and chips, I'm ruined for life. I'll never be able to eat at Captain Clancey's in Orlando again."

I smiled and took another bite of the crisp, battered fish. Good stuff.

"So, I realize this is probably a pointless question, but what do you want to do tomorrow?" Kellie asked.

"I picked up one of each of the sightseeing brochures from the hotel, but I haven't looked at them yet." I wiped off my oily fingers and fanned the stack of brochures like a deck of cards. "We could play Go Fish."

"I'd rather eat the fish."

"Then just pick a card, any card."

"Are you going to do a magic trick for me?"

"The only magic trick would be if we actually ended up doing whatever is on the brochure."

"Okay." Kellie reached across the table, closed her eyes, and pulled out one of the brochures.

"Let's see the winning card."

She held up a brochure with a picture of a hot-air balloon soaring over the Cotswolds. The grin on her face was enormous.

Ten

"No," I said resolutely as Kellie waved the hot-air balloon brochure in front of me. "No, no, no."

"What do you mean? I picked this one fair and square. Don't you think this would be fun?"

"No."

Kellie laughed. "I do. I've always wanted to go up in a hot-air balloon. Do you remember the year I got the new dishwasher for Mother's Day?"

I nodded, not sure what that had to do with anything at the moment. "I was at your house the day the old monster erupted. I helped you sop up the flood, remember?"

"That's right. You were there that Saturday. That was the first year I told Martin I wanted to go on a hot-air balloon ride for Mother's Day. I know Martin checked into a couple of companies in Orlando, but finances being what they were for us during those years, and the timing of the dishwasher's death—"

"You got a new dishwasher instead." I frowned. "Sorry, I finished your sentence for you. I'm not trying to turn into Opal or Rose."

Kellie laughed. "Don't worry. We're not there quite yet. And if we are on our way to becoming like the two of them, who cares? Finishing each other's sentences is part of the ebb and flow of being us."

"Which one do you want to be?"

"Which what do I want to be, Liz?"

"Ebb or Flo? Which one do you want to be?"

Kellie laughed again. "I'll be Ebb."

"Then I'll be Flo," I said, glad to have distracted her from the hot-air balloon topic.

"And since we're in England," Kellie said, "we really should consider elevating our status to Lady Ebb and Lady Flo."

It was a good thing we were in a noisy pub because we started practicing our British accents and quickly cracked each other up. Although Kellie and I grew louder and sillier by the minute, our antics seemed to go unnoticed by those around us.

"Now, back to the topic on the table," Kellie said. "What do you think, Lady Flo? A hot-air balloon ride in the morning?"

"Or perhaps," I said, reviewing the brochure on top of the untried stack, "we might consider a gentle punt down the River Cherwell, dear Lady Ebb. Here." I fanned out the rest of the brochures on the table like paint chips, hoping to entice her into a different selection.

Kellie flipped through the brochure in her hand. "It says here, my dear Lady Flo, that they pick us up at our hotel, and the whole escapade takes four hours. We need to be ready to go at 6:00 a.m. We could be ready by then, don't you think?"

I didn't answer. Kellie looked at my tense expression.

"Why, my dear Lady Flo, whatever is the matter?"

"I have a small preference for gravity over hot air."

She laughed and switched to her normal voice. "You just defied gravity on the plane ride here, remember? Over the Atlantic Ocean, I might add."

"I know."

She looked at me with her chin lowered, and her eyes lit up as if she had superhuman x-ray powers to read my mind. "You're serious, aren't you? The thought of floating up into the air while being supported by nothing more than a wicker basket and the reputation of a hot-air balloon pilot unnerves you."

I gave her a thanks-a-lot look. "Yes, it does. Especially when you put it that way."

Kellie laid the brochure on the table. "So what is your idea of how to spend a fabulous morning in Oxford? Or are you thinking we should set out as early as we can for London?"

"I'd like to spend a little time here in the morning. I was thinking it would be great to check out a bookstore to see if I could find one of my favorite classics. That would be ideal." I didn't conclude my thought aloud, but never on any list would I add "hot-air balloon ride" under the heading of "What to Do in Oxford."

"Okay, we can do that."

I caught just the edge of disappointment in my friend's expression.

"You really want to do this, don't you?" I picked up the brochure. "Maybe you should do it, then."

"I think we should both do this. It will be so much more fun if we go together. Besides, isn't it 'always friendlier with two'? At least that's what I read in a piece of British literature."

"In what book does that line appear?"

"*Winnie-the-Pooh.*"

"Which A. A. Milne book? *The House at Pooh Corner* or—"

"Okay, okay, I confess." Kellie raised a hand to stop me. "I read it once on a Winnie-the-Pooh calendar. But the philosophy is still solid. It is friendlier with two. Especially when we're trying daring new adventures together."

"Why don't we head back to the hotel, then? We'll have to call to see if they have anything available in the morning."

"Does this mean you're thinking about it?"

I nodded. "Yes, I'm thinking about it." In the same way I told her I would think about going into business with her as K & L Interiors, I also was willing to think about the hot-air balloon ride. And in the same way I was already ninety-nine percent convinced that going into business together was too great a risk to our friendship, this "flight of fancy" was too risky for my comfort level. If Kellie needed to go up in that hot-air balloon tomorrow morning, I wouldn't stop her. But I didn't need to go up with her. I could enjoy the experience just as well from the ground, watching and waving. I didn't mention that to her in the pub, though. I really didn't want to burst her, uh, balloon.

Walking back to our hotel and still feeling a little punchy, I suggested we further our imitation of the regal versions of Opal and Rose by drawing back our shoulders, lifting our chins, and dauntlessly giving a stately nod to every person we passed as if they were the loyal subjects of our shire.

Opal and Rose had received loyal adoration from the entire township when they strolled their royal mile. Kellie and I received two smirks, one cackle, and three raised eyebrows. One woman we passed had two nicely curved raised eyebrows. The swarthy gent with her had one continuous eyebrow across both eyes. Hence, the three-eyebrow salute.

"I believe we were well received," Kellie said as we arrived back at the hotel.

"Hot pink trainers would have helped us draw a little more attention, though."

The attendant at the front desk didn't look amused with our boisterous entrance, but she did help Kellie make the phone call to the hot-air balloon company to set up the plans.

"Okay, all set!" Kellie announced a few minutes later. "We'll need a wake-up call at five o'clock, and a guy named Jeremy will be here at six to 'collect' us."

"Do you prefer tea or coffee?" the front desk attendant asked.

"Tonight?"

"No, in the morning. For your wake-up call we send one of our servers up to your room with a morning beverage and a basket of breads."

"How nice. I'd like tea. Liz, what would you like?"

"Tea, of course." I had become a tea convert rather quickly. I appreciated the way the tea taste lingered in my mouth without the acidic aftertaste coffee had.

A half hour later Kellie hopped into bed, and before I had turned off the light, I could tell by her steady breathing that she was off in dreamland, probably floating through the clouds.

I was having a harder time falling asleep. I thought about why we had ended up in Oxford. Was it possible God had directed us to the wrong bus so we could have all these experiences? Was He the one who directed us to the crazy cabby so we could have a knock-our-socks-off tour of sites in Oxford that we never would have seen otherwise?

Possibly.

No. The more I thought about it, the correct answer was "probably." Probably this was God's idea all along. He was leading us. All the jumbled, unexpected events that had come to us since we had arrived were gifts from our heavenly Father. Both of us had prayed last week during the planning stages that God would lead us. We just never expected Him to lead in such unusual ways.

Even though none of this trip was going the way I had thought it would, it was way beyond my simple hopes. My expectations had been along the lines of viewing the Crown Jewels, visiting an art museum, and seeing a play. Yet this, too, was England. All of it. We were savoring a rare taste of so much more than the average visitor gets to experience. It struck me that God was "gracing" us with more than we ever imagined. I had a wish to go to England so I could see Big Ben; my expectations were small. God's gifts to us were immense.

The realization humbled me.

I readjusted my position under the covers and thought of how, just as God had given me my wish to go to England, He now seemed to be offering Kellie her wish of a hot-air balloon ride, and she wanted me to take a risk and go with her.

An image floated into my thoughts of Opal popping out of her chair that morning and setting the pace for her own happy little pancake race. Then I thought of Rose and her weighty stares of disapproval.

I drew in a deep breath and glanced across the shadowed room at peaceful Kellie. She wanted to go up in the hot-air balloon. With me.

Okay. Why not? Up, up, and away. No anchors from this best friend.

After I made that determination, I nodded off and slept wonderfully well.

A tap on the door at five the next morning produced a shy young woman who carried in a tray with a pot of tea and two cups with saucers. The tray also had a small pitcher of milk and a dish with sugar cubes. The basket of assorted breads steamed with the warmth of the fresh bakery items. She placed the tray on the end table between our two beds and slipped out as Kellie and I roused from a deep slumber.

"Such service," I said.

"I feel like royalty. Breakfast in bed!"

"May I pour you a spot of tea, Lady Ebb?"

"Oh, yes please, would you, Lady Flo? You are so kind."

"Oh, yes, aren't I, though?"

We sipped our tea while still in bed and shared some petite muffins tucked in the white cloth napkin that lined the basket.

"Kellie, I decided last night that I want to do this with you. I want to defy gravity and go up in the hot-air balloon."

Kellie's expression lines were curling up in the happiest sort of way.

Just then we heard a soft tapping on our door.

"Yes?" I called out.

"A message came for you this morning. Shall I slip it under the door?"

"Yes, thank you." I shot a wary glance at Kellie. No one knew we were at this hotel. Who would leave a message for us?

Kellie scanned the note. "It's from the hot-air balloon company. Due to a schedule adjustment, our launch time has been postponed. They will pick us up at nine. Well, we might as well check out the local bookstores if they're open."

A short time later, with a map in hand and wearing several layers of clothes, we headed down the street in the same direction we had taken toward the pub the night before. The skies were clear, and the air was crisp. Sunshine came gallantly marching through the narrow spaces between the old buildings and left its footprints on the cobblestones. We could see our breath as we walked briskly, trying to warm up.

"It's a gorgeous day," I said. "I love this early morning light."

The first open shop we saw was a used bookstore. It seemed early in the day for a shop to be open, but as Kellie reminded me, "This is a college town. Students need books at all hours of the day and night."

Ducking inside, we were met head-on with the scent of old books laced with a hint of pipe tobacco. The shelves reached to the ceiling in the small shop. All the books that hadn't found a place to perch on one of the shelves were stacked in precarious leaning towers at the end of each aisle. In the far corner of the small shop, an old cane-back chair awaited weary book hunters alongside a crook-necked lamp wearing an amber shade at a fashionable slant. The invitation to sit in the corner and read was a dusty sort of invitation, but welcoming nonetheless.

We shopped in separate sections of the curious little bookstore. I picked up books as if they were shells washed ashore after a storm on a deserted beach. Everything about the atmosphere in that used bookshop made me want to be smart. It felt as if millions of particles of knowledge were swirling around in the air. If I stood there long enough, some of them might land on me, sink inside, and enliven my brain cells.

"I want to learn something," I whispered, coming up next to Kellie.

"Like what?"

"I don't know. Something new. Something in the field of botany or Russian history or astrophysics. Well, maybe not astrophysics."

She smiled.

"Doesn't this place make you feel like a student? It makes me feel like I should engage my thoughts in something new and profound."

"I felt that way yesterday when we popped our heads into the Rabbit Room at the Eagle and Child. I hoped maybe I could catch some of Tolkien's and Lewis's leftover imagination particles," Kellie said.

I saw she had a book in her hand. "What are you buying?"

She held up the cover so I could see her find. It was a well-used copy of J. R. R. Tolkien's *The Hobbit.* "For Braden," she said. "He'll love that the book came from Oxford. What about you?"

"Just a few treasures." I showed her my four books: Shakespeare's *Twelfth Night,* Sir Arthur Conan Doyle's Sherlock Holmes novel *The Hound of the Baskervilles,* Charlotte Brontë's *Jane Eyre* in a 1947 hardback edition, and Sir Walter Scott's lengthy poem *The Lady of the Lake* in a pocket-sized version.

"Nice assortment," she said. "All your British authors."

"Yes. Well, Scott was from Scotland, but the rest were from England."

With our treasures paid for and wrapped in brown butcher paper and tied with a string by the clerk, Kellie and I stepped back outside into the chilly sunshine. Kellie had also purchased a map of Oxford, which she already had opened.

"Where to now?" I asked.

"I was trying to find Exeter College. That's where Tolkien taught, if I remember what the cab driver said. It looks like it's this way." She pointed to the left.

"Are you sure, Lady Ebb?"

She gave me a smirk. "Would you rather take a taxi?"

"I don't think we can afford to take another taxi the rest of the trip after what yesterday's gallivanting cost us."

"Then let's walk. It will warm us up on this invigorating day." Kellie picked up the pace. "Have you ever felt the air this crisp on your face at home?"

"No, never. I love it. I just wish I had bought a warmer coat." I noticed we were no longer strolling. We were women on a mission. Kellie took us around a bend, down an alleyway, and out onto a wide street with lots of cars and buses and an intersection with traffic stopped in both directions. It was by far the widest street we had seen in Oxford. The traffic light didn't appear to be working. All the vehicles were taking their turns at hedging their way across the no man's land in the middle.

"We have to be getting close." Kellie huffed and puffed as our power walk continued past more bookshops, woolen clothing stores, and a coffee shop alive with morning coffee drinkers and a table set up outside on the narrow sidewalk. Most of the shop's patrons looked like they were college age.

More students brushed past us. I smiled, imagining that some of the learning they had been stuffing into their brains might be leaking out and was therefore ready to light on the nearest head—mine!

We turned a corner, and a large number of students were funneling into a small opening in a tall stone wall.

"I think this is it," Kellie said.

"Should we follow them?"

"What? Pretend we're students?"

"Why not? We can go back to pretending we're Lady Ebb and Lady Flo, if you want."

With chins forward, we entered the stream of students passing through the creamy-colored, block-wall entry and into the courtyard. No one stopped us as we walked through the entrance. The sensation of sneaking in was delicious.

Eleven

Inside, behind the high wall surrounding Exeter College, lay a manicured lawn in a large rectangle surrounded by a walkway. The antiquated buildings that encased the courtyard were three stories high and crafted from pitted sandstone that gave the buildings a soft, buttery color in the morning light.

The students all seemed to be headed for the classrooms inside the rectangular buildings. None of them was going to the more ornate building on our left. It looked like a chapel, with tall, arched windows and a pitched roof. We took several steps up and were greeted by organ music. We inched forward, wanting to make sure a service wasn't in progress.

The organ music suddenly stopped, and so did our footsteps. We paused, looking at each other, wondering if we had been found out.

"Begin again, if you please. From the last bar," a distant voice above us said. The organ music, emanating from the chapel's back balcony, started up again. We couldn't see the master or the student, and we didn't think they could see us. But we could certainly hear them, and if Kellie and I got too loud, they would be able to hear us.

But we weren't loud. We were as reverent and tippytoey as church mice. All we wanted was a quick peek. And, oh boy, did we get what we came for!

The long, narrow chapel was the most beautiful and intricately decorated either of us had ever seen. The elevated pews were positioned on the right and left sides, leaving the center aisle open and the front of the chapel ablaze with breathtaking, soaring, stained-glass windows. The sunshine lit up all the vibrant colors in the stained glass, and dozens of images of biblical accounts danced before us, highlighted with heavenly brilliance. Kellie and I stood with our hands folded in front of us as we tried to take it all in. It was much more exalted than the simple sandstone country chapel Lewis attended that we had visited yesterday.

I felt awe and reverence. The chapel didn't seem overdone or gaudy. I loved the arched ceilings, the dark wood, and the artistic balance of all the elements. Someone who loved details had decorated this chapel. More likely it had been decorated and redecorated many times over the hundreds of years of its existence. One could sit here and worship Creator God for years and never notice all the intricacies in the tapestries or the small details in the carvings on the pews.

Cautiously I took several steps into the worship area, then paused behind a wooden lectern that held a large Bible. Affixed to the front of the pulpit was a glimmering bronze eagle with its wings back and its face to the altar. With my hands now clasped behind my back, I saw that the large Bible was open in about the middle of Jeremiah. I scanned the verses before me, curious if the Bible was only for display or if it was actually read from during a service.

I tried to imagine what it would sound like to hear God's Word read aloud in this jewel case of a chapel. Would the words, read in a rich British accent, match the beauty of the stained glass and the deep hue of the carved pews?

Squaring my shoulders, I tried out a sample reading in a low voice, using my best British accent. The organ practice in the balcony behind me certainly would drown out my reading.

"Jeremiah chapter 24, verse 7. 'I will give them hearts that will recognize me as the LORD. They will be my people, and I will be their God, for they will return to me wholeheartedly.'"

The organ struck a major chord and held it. I smiled. This was good stuff. I was beginning to develop an affection for the majesty built into the worship in a formal "high church" setting that wasn't always evident in the more casual church we attended. What did Opal call it? A contemporary service?

I liked our church and the familiarity of it. I wasn't interested in changing. But I felt a growing curiosity over what it would be like to worship in a place like this chapel. The verse I had just read felt richer, somehow, reading it here.

Double-checking the reference, I decided I would mark that same Jeremiah passage in my Bible so I could always remember what it felt like to read it here.

Kellie had wandered off to the side where she was scanning a tapestry hanging between two marble pillars. I stepped closer, and she turned to me with the look of a treasure hunter on her face.

"Morris," she whispered. "I'm sure of it. It has to be an original. Lizzie, look at the shape of the birds and the way the vines intertwine. And the choice of colors. I can't believe I'm looking at an original Morris!"

I whispered back, "Do you want to take a picture of it?"

"Do you think it's okay?"

We glanced around. No signs indicated otherwise. Kellie pulled out her camera and snapped three pictures.

The organ music stopped. Had they heard us whispering? Seen the camera flash? The pause sounded louder than the music had been.

With a mutual nod toward the door, we took our leave of the beautiful sanctuary. On our way out, the organ began again with the same piece.

I was already beyond the door when I noticed Kellie wasn't behind me. I saw a flash and peered back inside to see Kellie take a picture of a bust in a small alcove and then turn to take a few final snaps of the inner chapel and the stained-glass windows.

When she stepped outside with me, her face glowed. "What an incredible chapel. Such a great balance in the colors. Didn't you love the tones of the wood and their contrast to the jewel tones in the stained-glass windows?"

I nodded, even though I hadn't taken it all in with the eye of an artist like Kellie had.

"I loved all the detail in the carving on every single column. I could spend an entire day in there. And did you see the bronzed bust I was photographing?"

"No, who was it?"

"Tolkien! This was such a treasure. I'm so glad the balloon ride was delayed and we got 'detoured' to Oxford."

"I thought about that a lot last night, and I'm convinced none of what has happened to us has been an accident. God is direct-ing us."

"I'll say. I've thought about that too. These past few days seem like they have to be God's idea because nothing, absolutely nothing, has gone the way we thought it would. And to be hon-est with you, I think it's gone better than anything we could have planned."

I agreed and told myself to remember this affirmation of God's sweet grace on us when it came time to step into the hot-air balloon's wicker basket. I repeated the admonition to myself an hour or so later as we were riding out into the Oxfordshire coun-tryside, heading for the Cotswolds. The driver of the minivan, Jeremy, was also our hot-air balloon pilot. I was thankful that nothing about our ride with him was wild. His wife, Andrea, had come with him and was on her cell phone, checking with the crew in the field.

I gazed out the window at the expanding view. At long last I had a chance to take in the English countryside. And what a glorious vista spread out before us! The low, rolling hills were dressed in that fresh shade of early spring green I was coming to adore.

"Look!" Kellie pointed out her side of the van. In a large field hemmed in by a low stone wall, a matronly speckling of ewes nibbled at the sprouting greens.

"Have you enjoyed your stay in Oxford?" Andrea asked as soon as she finished her phone call.

"Yes, it's a wonderful place," I said. "It seems like it would take years to see it all."

Andrea chuckled. "Not years, I'd say. A few weeks, perhaps."

"Yesterday we had a wild time." Kellie started an Ebb and Flo summary of our crazy tour with the questionable cabby.

Jeremy and Andrea exchanged looks of surprise. Andrea interrupted us and said, "You went on the Peeping Jon Tour!"

"Peeping Jon?"

"The cab driver's name is Jon, and the local news ran a story on him last week. He was described as the self-appointed tour guide who walks sightseers right up to the windows of Lewis's and Tolkien's homes to have a look inside. Everyone is up in arms about it because Lewis's home is owned by a foundation and has regularly scheduled study groups that stay there. Tolkien's home is a private residence."

"We definitely didn't peek in anyone's windows," I said. At the same time, I felt a little as if we had been part of a paparazzi brigade, snapping pictures of lawn gnomes and grave sites. I couldn't imagine how awkward it would have been if the cabby had taken us to the crematorium or hospital. Did visitors actually take pictures of those places?

"Did you leave everything as you found it?" Jeremy asked.

"Yes. Of course," Kellie said.

"Some tourists have been trying to take bricks from Lewis's fence and shingles from Tolkien's home. It's maddening."

"You have to understand what's happened here," Andrea said. "Ten years ago you could have asked anyone on the street who Lewis was, and they wouldn't have known. Now, with the success of the *Narnia* and *Lord of the Rings* films, as well as the fact that parts of *Harry Potter* were filmed here, well, Oxford suddenly is swarming with a different sort of tourist than we've had before."

Jeremy said, "You can see how it's off-putting to the neighbors and such. Last thing anyone wants is a Hollywood-style touring coach to come rumbling down the street every hour loaded with tourists and their cameras."

"Although we do love tourists, don't we, Jeremy?" Andrea stated quickly.

"Right. Tourists like Kellie and Liz. That's what we like. I guess we're a bit snooty in that way."

We returned Andrea's quick grin over her shoulder. A few minutes later Jeremy pulled into an open field and parked behind a large truck. On my side of the minivan stood a long row of poplars in their minimalist garb after being stripped down by winter's merciless blast. At the edge of the field a team of men were unfurling what looked like an enormous bright orange and blue tarp.

Kellie took one look at the wicker basket waiting to the side of the flattened balloon and seemed to have second thoughts. "How do all of us fit in that tiny basket?"

"It's larger than it looks," Andrea said.

"If there's only room for one of us…," I began.

I could tell Kellie was checking my vitality signs. I smiled confidently so she wouldn't think I was wimping out on her. I was merely being hospitable.

"There's room for both of you as well as Jeremy. The rest of us are on the chase team," Andrea said. "We'll follow you in the truck and pick you up where the balloon comes down for a landing."

"So where will we land?"

Andrea grinned. "The air currents make that decision for us, and I'll tell you: it's never the same place twice. Jeremy is very good at catching just the right current, and often he can maneuver the balloon in the direction he wants it to go. Not always, but most of the time."

"Don't worry," Jeremy called over his shoulder to us. "It will be fine. Today is an excellent day to go up, even though this is later than we usually launch."

Jeremy gave a nod to one of the men already on the field who was working on unfurling the balloon. "We haven't lost a tourist yet, have we, Sven?"

"Not yet," Sven answered.

"Have you been doing this long?" I asked Sven, shading my eyes from the sun with my forearm.

With a professional tone, he stood a little straighter. "Your flight will be my second one."

I turned to Andrea with a stunned expression on my face.

"He's putting you on," Andrea said. "This is his third year with us. Before he moved to England, he worked on a cruise ship. We think the time at sea did something to his gray matter."

I stood to the side and watched the team prepare the balloon for flight. Kellie and I were soon called on to assist during the inflating. We each were given a pair of gloves and assigned a side of the long balloon. Our job was to keep an eye on the fabric now laid out on the field to make sure the balloon filled unhindered with air from a large fan run by a generator.

We took our places. The sudden noise as the fan whirled into action in the peaceful countryside sent a flock of black birds out of their grazing spot in the field. They took flight looking like two dozen black dots that all hung together as a unit. The many individuals comprised a whole flock as long as they stuck together. It was beautiful watching them swoop and soar in harmony.

I was watching the birds when I should have been watching my side of the balloon.

"Give it a tug!" Jeremy called over the rumble of the fan. "Gently!"

I bent over to straighten the fabric and felt something no one ever wants to feel. The seat of my jeans gave way. They were my oldest and most comfortable pair, which is why I had brought them on the trip. I had no idea they were worn all the way to the threads.

I snapped straight up and tried to assess the damage without appearing too obvious. I looked right and left as well as behind me. The others were busy with the balloon's inflation. I slipped out of my sweater and casually tied it around my waist so my backside was covered. Stepping back, I gazed in awe as the massive balloon filled with air and seemed to come to life like a bobbing float from the Macy's Thanksgiving Day Parade.

I strode around to Kellie's side of the billowing beast, then leaned over and said, "I ripped my jeans."

"No! Did you really?"

"I wouldn't make up something like that at a time like this."

"I have a little sewing kit in my bag. Let's go back to the van. I can sew them up for you there."

Trotting after her I said, "Did I ever tell you how much I appreciate your organizational skills?"

"Yes. But you can tell me again if you want."

"I appreciate your organizational skills. I just wish my dieting skills were as successful as your organizational skills."

Kellie laughed the way a best friend is supposed to laugh when you're humiliated and at a loss for what to do or say. The only protection at such a time is a clever attempt at a joke. And such attempts only work if your best friend laughs with you the way Kellie did just then.

We settled into the van's backseat and made it look as if we were simply Lady Ebb and Lady Flo, two women of refinement who preferred waiting in the car rather than out in the fray of all the flight preparations.

I wiggled out of my worn jeans while Kellie scrounged for her travel-sized sewing kit.

"Oh, rats," she said.

"What do you mean, 'oh, rats'? I'm sitting here in my undies, a few feet away from a male flight crew, and you say, 'oh, rats'?"

Kellie held up a complimentary hotel-type sewing kit the size of a matchbook. The edges were crumpled, and it looked as if it had been in her purse a long time. "I have thread, but the needle is gone. I must have used it before."

"Kellie!"

"I know. Rats, huh? Would you like me to ask Andrea if she has a sewing kit or first-aid kit or something?"

"I guess. Whatever you do, be quick about it because it's feeling a little breezy in here."

Kellie slipped out and hurried over to Andrea. I wrapped my jeans around my bare legs and put my sweater back on. Then I sat on my hands in an effort to keep them warm. From the confines of the car, I could see Jeremy checking the thick ropes that tethered the basket and its inflatable bonnet. They were going to be ready to launch soon.

"Come on, come on, come on, come on," I murmured, watching Kellie as she talked to Andrea and pointed back at the car. Sven seemed to be listening in.

"Don't tell the whole world, Kellie, please!"

Andrea shook her head. This wasn't looking good. My guess was needles weren't something people in the balloon business often carried.

I was about to slip my jeans back on and use my sweater once again for camouflage when I noticed Sven jogging over to the car.

"No! Go away! Oh dear. I don't have time to get my jeans on! Sven, be gone!"

I tucked my jeans around my bare legs as completely as I could, then I sat up straight in a tense pose and prepared myself for the Swedish invasion.

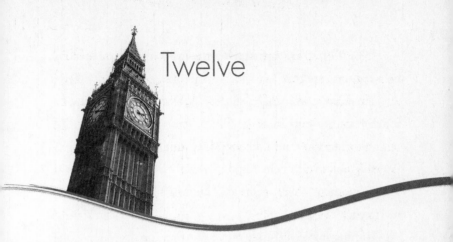

Twelve

Sven tapped on the van's closed window in a gesture of politeness before sliding open the side door. A blast of cool air caused goose bumps to run up and down my bare legs.

"May I offer some assistance?" He kept his eyes strategically on my face. I thought his approach was odd until I remembered Andrea saying he had worked on a cruise ship. He probably had opened a lot of doors in the midst of unusual circumstances.

"I think I'll be okay. Thanks."

"You might want to try this." Sven held up the universal answer to fix whatever is broken. "Duct tape."

"Okay. Thanks. I'll give it a try."

Kellie was back at the van and saw me holding the duct tape. Sven walked away. She climbed in and closed the door. "Lizzie, I'm not trying to be negative, but don't you think a nice, wide silver stripe up your backside is going to be noticeable?"

"Not if I put the duct tape on the inside of my jeans. Here, help me measure this."

"Ah. Clever woman," Kellie said. "Did I ever tell you how much I admire your creative skills?"

"No, and I'm not in the mood for you to start now."

She took my grouchy response exactly as she should have at such a moment—with a shrug. The task at hand was all that mattered.

Turning my jeans inside out, I saw that the rip wasn't along the seam. It was an uneven tear in the fabric. These jeans were more worn out than I had realized. They were ready to be tossed. But not yet. I needed them to hold together for a few more hours.

After affixing several strips of tape to the inside of my jeans, I smoothed each piece into place on the denim and then wiggled back into the repaired jeans.

"Now I'm going to get out of this van, and I'm going to sashay over to the hot-air balloon. I have only one favor to ask."

"Sure, anything. What is it?"

"If you have any affection for me, I beg of you, Kellie, do not look at my backside. Do not make comments about my backside while I'm walking. Do not try to touch or otherwise adjust my backside. Okay?"

"Okay." Kellie nodded, but I could tell she was dying to let loose with a few witty lines. Thankfully, she kept her quips to herself.

Trying to regain whatever regal composure I had left when I entered the car, I disembarked and gave a slight wiggle to adjust my repaired britches before walking over to the waiting balloon. Andrea, Jeremy, Sven, and the other three men were all waiting, holding on to the tethered ropes. All of them were smiling broadly, but none made eye contact with me.

I gathered myself and focused on the wicker basket, which looked even smaller now that the balloon was mounted above it. The balloon still was filling with hot air expelled from a unit that shot intense flames up into the expanding space. The balloon was a beautiful, colorful, fat, King Kong–sized monster, looming high and wide above that small basket. And here we were, on the threshold of Kellie's wish.

Jeremy clambered into the basket first and then held out his hand to me. I was supposed to climb up on a box and step over the edge of the basket onto another box and then find my place to stand inside the basket. Easy.

Only my feet didn't move. "Kellie, you want to go first?"

"No, go ahead, Liz. I've got your back…" She wisely didn't finish her sentence.

This was harder than I thought it would be. I told my pounding heart to calm down and just enter into the moment. This was a rare opportunity. This was Kellie's wish.

And we already had paid for it.

"I'll tell you now, there is no dainty way to go aboard," Andrea said loudly over the roar of the flame shooting into the cavernous belly of Kong. She was standing to the side, holding one of the thick tethering ropes with gloved hands. "Just swing one leg over the edge, and you'll be in good shape."

With one foot in front of the other, I climbed up on the box. Then, trying to steady myself, I held on to the edge of the basket.

Jeremy adjusted the flame, and the air went astonishingly still.

Kellie had honored my request not to mention or draw attention to my backside all the way across the field. However, it seemed she couldn't resist offering a single line at the precise moment that I followed Andrea's advice and looped my right leg into the basket.

"I guess it's true. Every cloud does have a silver lining."

I tried to ignore her, but my smile broke through, and I let a nervous flutter of embarrassed laughter tumble into the basket before I did. And tumble is the key word. My footing wasn't secure, and I'm sure I came close to dislocating Jeremy's arm as I tried to steady myself. Once I had both feet firmly in the basket, I laughed myself silly.

I looked at Kellie just impishly enough to let her know I would get her back later. In the sweetest way possible, of course.

Jeremy directed me where to stand, and I took my small, small place as compactly as I could. He put one hand on the controls that regulated the on-and-off switch for the blaze and made an adjustment.

The flame kicked up again with a mighty roar.

"Next." Jeremy held out his hand to Kellie. She took the first step up, grasped his forearm, and managed to climb over the wicker rampart without too much trouble. I'm not saying it was a pretty entrance, but it was controlled, swift, and much more elegant than mine.

"Show-off," I muttered playfully.

"Actually, I think your show was much better than mine. Acrobatics are always a crowd pleaser."

Before I could continue the banter, we started going up. We were moving slowly, as if we were in an elevator. We were leaving the earth below us, defying gravity, and making a smooth ascent. The moment was thrilling.

I looked over at Kellie. She was beaming.

Below us, Andrea waved.

Kellie waved back. I just held on and smiled.

The flame in the center of the basket seemed like a supersized Bunsen burner. Jeremy turned it off. All was calm. We kept floating upward. The sensation wasn't so much that we were moving but that the earth was pulling away from us.

The world around us was strikingly silent. We heard a lamb bleat from a field far below, and the sound was so crisp and clear it seemed as if the lamb were only a few feet away.

"It's so quiet," Kellie whispered.

Jeremy nodded. "That's the first thing everyone says."

"How can we be moving?" Kellie asked. "It feels like the breeze stopped."

"We're moving with the air currents."

"This is amazing," Kellie cooed. "What a sensation of tranquillity."

Kellie and I stood with our feet firmly planted in the basket, taking in the expanding view of the countryside below us. The field had transformed into a dusty green patchwork quilt. Low stone walls formed straight lines between the patches. White, woolly sheep dotted some of the squares and rectangles of land. They became smaller and smaller as we rose above it all. It felt as if we were floating along in a raft on a calm river, only instead of water, the air current provided the silent river on which we bobbed.

All my apprehensions, real and imagined, seemed to have stayed behind on planet Earth. We were free birds, soaring above it all. I felt that initial taste of victory, such as when I'm trying a new recipe for company, and it seems everything is turning out the way it's supposed to.

The burner fired up again. Kellie and I both flinched. We smiled at each other and then smiled at Jeremy as if to tell him we had made peace with the dragon's breath. We needed the bellowing beast's fire at its unexpected intervals to keep us aloft. We rose and caught a different current that floated us toward a small pond. At least from our vantage point it appeared to be a small pond. As we gently were lowered back to earth, the pond became larger.

"On some rides I've been able to lower the basket so that we skim the water. But don't worry; I don't plan to try it today." Jeremy fired up the heat, and we rose. When all was quiet again he said, "The currents aren't usually so cooperative this time of day. We generally go up in the morning or the evening if it's warm enough. This is an exceptional day."

"Yes, it is an exceptional day," Kellie agreed. "What beautiful countryside."

I didn't have the words right then to describe everything my eyes as well as my other senses were taking in. *Beautiful* didn't begin to cover it.

"My camera!" Kellie reached into her coat pocket. "I almost forgot I brought it."

"I get copies of all your pictures, okay?" At the moment I wasn't sure where I had left my camera, and I wasn't going to let go of the basket's edge to search my coat.

"Smile for me, Liz!" Kellie took dozens of digital shots. Jeremy took several of both of us and then a few of Kellie by herself, her expression still lit up like a child's on Christmas morning.

I stood in my spot inside the basket, feeling as stable as if I were standing on a cement slab. Taking in a 360-degree view, I soaked it all in. We floated up and down and over a blissful corner of God's green Earth.

The peaceful sensation was lulling. All we had to do was float. The effortlessness of our movement calmed me and made me wonder what I'd been so afraid of when Kellie had suggested this last night. What a tragedy it would have been if I had missed the moment. Risk has its rewards, and today the reward was a sumptuous feast for all the senses.

We could tell our amazing ride on the air currents was concluding as the land below us seemed to rise up to meet us with open arms. Andrea and the others in the chase vehicle waited at the edge of a different field than the one we had taken off from. She waved as we descended, and we could hear clearly every word she and the guys were saying. It was a strange sensation.

As the earth steadily drew closer, I felt the instinct to brace myself for the crash. Jeremy had assured us he could land us without crashing. "We may experience a few bumps, though," he said.

I counted only two bumps, along with an overt swaying back and forth before our spacecraft came to a stop. Then it was over. I didn't want to get out.

But with a little help from the crew, Kellie and I both managed to make commendable exits. Not graceful, but not worth the price of a circus ticket either.

"I have to sit down." I plopped onto the grass.

"Do your legs feel wobbly?" Andrea asked.

"A little. I just feel…"

"Awed?" Kellie concluded for me.

"Yes, awed."

She sat beside me, and we grinned at each other. Kellie said, "That was so…"

"Incredible?" I ventured.

"Yes. Incredible and peaceful. I loved it." She turned to

Andrea and Jeremy. "Thanks so, so much. This was my wish for a long time."

"That makes it all the better," Andrea said. "It's been our pleasure. I'll drive you back to the hotel when you're ready. Jeremy and the crew are meeting another party shortly."

"We're ready whenever you are," Kellie said.

I rose from the grass first, and Kellie followed. The two of us said our farewells and thank-yous to Jeremy, Sven, and the crew, and then we walked across the field to the van.

"Uh, Lizzie?" Kellie called out from her position behind me. "I know I promised I wouldn't make a comment about…"

"I know. It's okay. I thought the silver lining joke was hilarious. Don't worry about it."

"Well, it's no longer just a silver lining. You have daisies on your…"

"What?" I gave the back of my torn jeans a brush with both hands and found that the sticky part of the duct tape had peeked through the rip and collected a bouquet of spring treasures. No, I didn't have daisies growing out of my backside, but I did have grass, clover, and a tiny weed of some sort with white leaves.

"Kellie!"

"What? Do you want me to help weed your portable little flower garden? Sorry, my acts of friendship only go so far."

I brushed off the remaining flora and fauna and called out to Andrea. "Don't bother taking us to the hotel. Take us directly to the first clothing store we come to."

Kellie chuckled. I glanced at her and knew she was dying to make another joke. By the shade of rose creeping up her neck, it was undoubtedly a good one.

"Go ahead," I said. "Spit it out."

"Are you sure?"

"Yes, I'm sure."

In a singsong voice she said, "I see London. I see France. I see someone's underpants."

If I hadn't been feeling still so humiliated, I would have laughed until I cried. It probably would have been good for me.

Instead of laughing with Kellie, I listed the flaws in her song. "I know my underwear isn't showing, and as for 'seeing London,' I'm beginning to doubt that is ever going to happen."

"Of course it's going to happen," Kellie said. "Come on. Our carriage awaits us."

I took the first step.

Kellie followed, singing out, "Duct, duct..." Then with a tag on my backside, she said, "Goose!" and took off running for the van.

I laughed so hard I thought I was going to rip the duct tape.

Thirteen

You know," Andrea said once the three of us were in the car, "according to ballooning tradition, first-time balloonists shake a bottle of champagne and pop it open when they land. Then they pick up a handful of dirt and rub it in their hair. Some balloonists keep that tradition alive with every first-time passenger."

"I'm glad you didn't include that tradition for our ride," I said. "I think I managed to muss myself up enough without spraying champagne or tossing any more earth around. And I was serious, by the way, about going shopping instead of going back to the hotel."

Andrea drove us to a rather upscale clothing store in Oxford. She graciously offered to wait for us in the car. I took a quick look around but didn't find anything I wanted to bother trying on.

Returning to the hotel, we thanked Andrea again for the memorable adventure. I changed into the other pair of pants I had brought, and Kellie and I managed to get ourselves to the train station and on the right train out of Oxford. At long last we were on our way to London.

"I'm starving," Kellie said soon after the train pulled out of the Oxford station. "Have we eaten anything today?"

"We had tea and those tiny muffins for breakfast."

"That was all, wasn't it? Is it teatime yet?"

"Your stomach already is thinking British. Tea does sound great right about now. I'll see if this train has a dining car or snack cart or something." Off I went, walking toward the caboose as the train moved forward. The sensation was similar to trying to walk up a downward moving escalator.

My sleuthing paid off with the discovery of a compact and sort of cute dining car that offered beverages and premade sandwiches. I bought an egg salad sandwich on white bread for us to split and two hot cups of tea.

When I returned to our seats, Kellie was bent over my compiled pages of London sights. She was making notes in the margins with her usual tiny printed letters. It was one of the many differences between us that we had friendly squabbles about. Kellie is nearsighted, while I am farsighted. I had to put on my reading glasses if I wanted to go over her notes.

"Thanks for the sandwich. This is perfect. I'm thinking we should take a taxi from the train station and go directly to the hotel. We could use the underground, but why hassle with the luggage?"

"I agree."

"We should be okay on our check-in time with the hotel. After we settle in our room, if you're still hungry, we could find a place to eat."

"Sounds good. What do you think about trying to make it to a play tonight?"

"I was looking at the information you pulled together. We have lots of options, but I'm thinking we should try to book tickets for a play either tomorrow night or maybe Saturday afternoon. That way we aren't so rushed."

I appreciated Kellie's organizational skills and her logic, but the truth was I did feel rushed, and I told her so.

"We have so much to see and do in London, and—I'm not complaining—but our first two days are gone. Not that I would have changed anything we've done or seen yesterday and today, it's just that…"

I kind of wanted Kellie to pull a Lady Ebb and finish my sentence for me. I wanted her to verbalize how behind we were on all the doing-and-seeing options listed on the papers in her lap.

Kellie didn't validate my panic, though. She took another bite of her sandwich and waited for me to complete my thought.

"There's so much," I concluded.

"So much what?"

"So much to see and do."

"Then we should prioritize," Kellie said. "Let's each pick our top five. Even if we only get to do or see two or three of our top five wonders of London in the next three days, we'll be doing great."

"Three days," I repeated, too glum to eat any more of the pasty egg-and-mayonnaise sandwich. "Why didn't we plan to stay longer?"

"Because Opal set the schedule, remember? We can accomplish a lot in three days if we organize ourselves."

I couldn't believe I was pouting. I was on a train bound for London, after having spent two incredible days in Oxford and Olney, but I was acting like a spoiled brat. "You know what? I'm not going to go glum over the shortness of our stay. Whatever we do here is going to be—"

"Fantastic."

"You're right, Kellie. Even if we went home right now, I would feel as if I had experienced the adventure of a lifetime."

"But we can't go home yet because of you-know-who."

"Who?"

"Your big crush."

"Oh, of course. You remembered." I smiled at the prospects waiting for us in the next few days. "My crush, Ben Baby. He's number one on my list."

"I thought so."

Skimming through the pages, Kellie and I took turns composing our lists. True to many other parts of our friendship, Kellie's list and mine were opposites. We had agreed years ago that opposites really did attract; our friendship was proof of that.

My top five were right out of a travel brochure for London:

Big Ben, Westminster Abbey, Buckingham Palace, Windsor Castle, and a play in the theater district.

"What did you come up with?" I asked Kellie.

"Portobello Road Market, Harrods, Crown Jewels at the Tower of London, Windsor Castle, and a museum."

"Which museum?"

"I'm not sure yet. According to your helpful research here, we can see Egyptian mummies at the British Museum, original Shakespeare scripts at the British Library, or Rembrandt self-portraits at the National Gallery."

"I know. It's like I said. There's so much to see and do."

"What I really want to see is Morris furniture and tapestries, but they weren't listed here, and I don't remember the name of the museum Rose and Opal said we should visit."

"The V and A," I said. "I think it was the Victoria and Albert Museum."

"Perfect! I just saw that one on this map. The Victoria and Albert Museum is practically across the street from Harrods department store."

Kellie and I combined our top must-sees, and she transferred them to a single list. Nice and tidy, just the way she liked things. We located each sight on a map, combined destinations, and tossed around runner-up choices. Our list of add-on adventures grew.

Kellie reminded me of our agreement to be flexible and let this trip unfold at its own pace. So far, nothing had gone the way I thought it would, but all of it had been wonderful.

I stepped back and let Kellie take the lead. She had all the information with her now. The hotel reservations were in her name. I didn't mind being the hunter-gatherer-turned-follower.

The train pulled into Paddington Station. We waited to be among the last off the train so we could get off without bumping into anyone with our wheeled luggage. A variety of commuters but no other tourists appeared to be in our train car. As we walked through the station, though, we saw lots of travelers, with bags of every sort and shape.

Kellie and I kept looking up at the high ceiling's design. Metal beams ran through the clear dome above us, creating the appearance of an elaborate series of wrought-iron veins.

"Do you remember the story of Paddington Bear?" I asked. "Both of my girls received stuffed Paddington Bears from my mother for Christmas one year."

"Is he the bear with the floppy hat and the luggage tag tied to his little raincoat?"

"That's Paddington. And this is his train station."

Outside we spotted a taxi stand and joined the line of three luggage-toting visitors. We had noticed a few times on our journey that people seemed to line up with the same amount of space between each person. It reminded me of being taught as a child to line up without "touching your neighbor." The only place where it seemed Brits hadn't lined up was at the bar in the pub. There I had noticed it was like moths to a porch light.

Within minutes we were loading our luggage into a traditional black cab, and Kellie was telling the driver where we wanted to go. We made ourselves comfortable on the wide seat across the back of the cab and noticed we had lots of open floor space in front of us for our luggage. Two folded-up jump seats were located on the back of the front bench seat directly across from us. I had never been in a vehicle with this sort of configuration. The other cabs we had ridden in so far were compact-sized cars that maneuvered well on the narrow streets of Olney and Oxford. If we didn't believe yet that we were actually in London, settling ourselves in this cab cinched it.

The streets were wide, the traffic was heavy, and on the sidewalks people were coming and going with purposeful strides. The buildings were a mix of old and new. Our driver zipped down and around a tangle of short streets in a residential area where huge trees lined up in a strip of grassy space that ran down the middle of the street. All the trees looked as if the millions of buds on their curving branches were about to burst open like popcorn and cover the naked winter limbs with an opulent show of white and pink pompoms.

"Doesn't this street feel like a scene from Dickens's *Oliver Twist*?" I asked.

"It's the Georgian-style architecture," Kellie said.

"Do you remember the film version of *Oliver*?"

"I think so."

"A scene takes place on a street just like this. Oliver opens the window at his grandfather's home, and a variety of peddlers start singing, 'Who will buy—'"

"Oh, look!" Kellie interrupted. We had turned onto a main thoroughfare, and red double-decker buses were motoring down both sides of the road. I had made sure my camera was in my jacket pocket, and I quickly pulled it out and snapped away.

"I didn't put the buses on our list," I said. "But we definitely need to ride a double-decker. Let's be sure to add that one."

"Got it." Kellie reached for the condensed list and pulled out her pen. "I thought of something else too."

"What's that?"

"Tea. We didn't put down to have tea someplace special, but I think it would be just lovely, don't you?"

A broad smile spread across my face. A Cheshire cat grin.

"What? Why are you smiling like that?"

"I'm smiling because I think going someplace special for tea is a wonderful idea." I attempted my best upper-class British accent. "Oh, yes, I can see it now: Lady Ebb and Lady Flo taking tea at the Ritz. How posh."

"Are you mocking my idea?"

"No, not at all. I love the idea of having tea at some extra special place. As a matter of fact, I love the idea so much that I have a little surprise for you."

Kellie gave me a wary look.

"It's a good surprise. When I was researching possible things to do, I had a feeling we would want to experience something swanky here in London. So I went online and booked a reservation for us to have tea at the Ritz Hotel. I thought it could be my early birthday present for you."

Kellie seemed as stunned and pleased as I had hoped she would. "Oh, Lizzie, I love it! Thank you."

"You're welcome. Several of the travel sites I checked recommended the Ritz Hotel but said their tea reservations book up months ahead. I was pretty excited that I was able to get a reservation for the only day they had open."

"What day?"

"Thursday."

"That's tomorrow!" Kellie glanced again at our roughly sketched-out schedule.

"I know. I've been trying to think of how to tell you. I wanted it to be a surprise. An early birthday treat you'll never forget."

"Believe me, I'll never forget any of this. How about if I act surprised once we show up at the tearoom?" She pulled out her pen. "Now, what time are the reservations?"

"Three o'clock."

Kellie looked up. "That seems a little early for tea. We've been imbibing closer to four o'clock."

"I know. Like I said, I was glad to get what I could."

"And I appreciate it. Tea at the Ritz. This is going to be so fun."

Our taxi driver turned into a circular driveway of a white Victorian-style building. It looked as if we were pulling into a grand museum entrance or a mansion. He stopped the cab, and I reached for Kellie's arm. "This is it? This is our hotel? We're staying here?"

"It's even better than all the pictures we looked at online."

"Kellie, this is way beyond what I had hoped for."

She didn't respond at the moment because she was busy settling the cab fare with our driver. The man hadn't said one word to us until now when he asked if Kellie needed a receipt. Actually, it had been refreshing to have a driver who didn't say a word after all the assistance we had received from our Oxford cab driver.

A bellman in a navy blue double-breasted uniform opened the cab door and greeted us. He was wearing a small pillbox-style hat with an elastic strap under his chin. In any other setting it would have looked odd. Here, it fit. All of it. The black taxicab, the uniformed bellman with the funny little hat, even the red carpet that beckoned us to follow it through revolving doors into a spacious hotel lobby.

The clerks at the front desk wore matching navy blue double-breasted jackets but no hats. Our receptionist was pleasant and helpful but a little confused when the reservation showed up as being cancelled for two nights in a row. As Kellie and I felt an oh-no cloud come over us, the supervisor showed the clerk how to bring up the adjusted reservation dates. Clearly the young woman was in training. I wondered how many young people came to London to work in an internship position like this at a nice hotel.

We were presented with two room keys slipped inside a folded card. Breakfast was complimentary, either downstairs in the restaurant or from the room service menu. The porter would deliver our luggage momentarily. If we would like to enjoy complimentary tea in the conservatory, we were welcome.

Kellie and I nodded "yes, thank you" to all the delicious invitations and then stepped away.

I was choked up. "Kellie, this is the nicest hotel I've ever stayed in. Tell your kind hubby thank you, thank you, thank you."

"You can tell him yourself if you like. I was thinking we should call home and check in tonight. What do you think?"

"Great idea." We both had called our first night at Rose's before going to bed. All was well with both Roger and Martin, and we had told them we would try to call again later in the week.

"But first, shall we have ourselves a cuppa?" Kellie used the term for a cup of tea that we had heard Opal use.

We seated ourselves in the opulently decorated conservatory area and were served steaming tea in individual-sized shiny silver pots. In front of us was placed a plate loaded with a selection of shortbread biscuits—cookies, to us—in various shapes. We loved the way they melted on our tongues.

Kellie and I sipped ourselves into happy oblivion. With sweetened up and seriously sloshing bellies, we found our way to our room, politely arguing all the way as to who got to use the bathroom facilities first.

Kellie backed down and let me go first after I whispered in the elevator that I had had my share of embarrassing moments for one day. She opened the door of our room, and we saw that our luggage had been delivered. I dashed into the modernized bathroom and was impressed with the luxurious-looking bathtub, the inset lighting, plush towels, and a generous assortment of toiletries on the marble counter.

Once Kellie and I were both standing in the middle of our room selecting beds, she said she was surprised that our room was so small, given the immensity of the lobby and conservatory. I thought the room was extravagant, but then my tastes and experiences in hotel rooms were more limited than Kellie's.

"I think this is fantastic." I opened the beautiful armoire and folded the doors back to reveal a television as well as a pullout tray with a hot pot and all the makings for tea. "If we need another cuppa, it looks like we have all the necessities right here."

Kellie walked over to the thick drapes, and with a "Ta-da!" she dramatically opened them. We both laughed. Our window faced an old wall that was dripping with moss. It was quaint having something so green growing right outside our window. The view certainly was unique.

"I think we'll keep the curtains closed," Kellie said. "What do you think?"

"Good idea." With that I flopped on the bed and smiled. We were in London at last.

Fourteen

I liked our room. I didn't mind not having a view. I thought the setup was perfect for us in every way. "So what do you want to do first?"

"Are you hungry?" Kellie asked.

"Are you kidding? Not after the two cups of tea we just had in the lobby and how many cookies did we eat?"

"Only five or six."

"Seven or eight, you mean."

"Hey, we're on vacation, Liz. Seven and eight are vacation numbers. They don't mean the same thing in foreign countries as they do at home. Time is different here, so why can't numbers be different too?"

I laughed. "So are you saying that eight cookies in England are equal to…"

"Two cookies of a similar kind in America," Kellie concluded.

"I like your logic."

"It's simple conversion, you know, like the way we have to convert the British pound into what it equals in U.S. dollars."

"We could call it 'travel math,'" I suggested.

"Hey, I like that! We should make up a chart. Such-and-such number in England is really equal to this number in the United States. And it will, of course, always be a lower number, like the difference between gallons and liters."

"Why not? Who needs the metric system? We have our own system. Travel math!"

Kellie and I got going, as we often did, and tried to out-pun each other with our new inside joke about reassigning the value of all calories with our travel math. The theory that eight tea biscuits equaled one Oreo gave us our first standard of measurement.

"You know"—I reached for my collection of travel info—"I'm not sure I printed it out, but while I was doing research, I found a chart online that said how to figure out your weight in the British system."

"It's not the same as our scales with pounds?"

"No, pounds is their money, remember?"

"Oh, that's right. So how do they weigh things?"

"In stones."

"You're kidding."

"No. I think the ratio is something like fourteen U.S. pounds on a weight scale is equal to one stone."

"Really? I could live with that."

"The drawback is that the shoe sizes start in the thirties and go up. I calculated my size before we came, and I wear a size forty shoe."

Kellie laughed. "So you're saying that with our travel math you weigh about eleven stone, and yet your feet won't fit into anything less than a forty shoe."

"You got it." In my best Ebb-and-Flo voice, I put on a little show for Kellie using my two hands as puppets. "'Good day, Lady Flo. How's your weight today?' 'Oh, Lady Ebb, I'm up to eleven today after that last biscuit.' 'Eleven, you say? That's a lovely number, don't you think?' 'Oh, not at all. I'm trying to get down to ten and half so I don't rip out the backside of my pants.' 'Oh, Lady Flo, you're such a kidder. That would never happen to you!'"

Kellie rolled over on her back on the bed and let out all her pent-up giggles. "Liz, you're such a good sport. I wish I had taken a picture of you walking around with those daisies on your behind!"

"They weren't daisies, and I wouldn't be speaking to you if you had taken a picture." I was trying to come across as indignant, but my efforts dissolved as soon as I remembered her "I see London" and "Duct, duct" jokes. My first chuckle was followed by a rush of giggles and guffaws that were egged on by Kellie laughing so hard she had to make another quick dash to the bathroom.

She called out, "Did you see this bathtub?"

"I know. It's a beauty, isn't it?"

"I'm going to take a bath."

"Good for you. I'm going to unpack." I could hear the water running as I pulled my clothes from my suitcase and placed them in the bottom drawer of the armoire. At the bottom of the suitcase was a travel-size Bible I had borrowed from Roger. He liked to take this Bible with him on the days he ushered because he could fit it in his pocket and keep both arms free for shaking hands and greeting people.

I paused and smiled, thinking of my Roger and how he loved ushering and greeting. I loved that he had found a place to serve at church for all these years.

I needed a place to serve. I didn't know what that would be, but it was time to give that serious consideration.

Taking Roger's Bible with me over to the corner of the room, I sank into the overstuffed chair and put my feet up on the hassock. In my familiar "hunt and gather" fashion, I went looking for the verse in Jeremiah I had read in the Exeter chapel.

"I will give them hearts that will recognize me as the LORD. They will be my people, and I will be their God, for they will return to me wholeheartedly."

The first part of the verse caught my attention. "Hearts that will recognize me as the LORD."

Copying the verse into my travel journal, I wondered if my heart truly recognized God as Lord. I had been saying that He was the One leading us on this trip. He was our true tour director. Was that another way of saying I recognized His hand in life's events? That He really was the Lord of this trip, of my whole life?

From the moment I had blown out the candles on my fifteenth birthday to this moment in a luxurious hotel with a moss-covered wall outside the window, did God know and see and plan all of it?

If so, then I had to ask why. Why would God care about the wishes of a fifteen-year-old girl? Why would He be so kind as to fulfill such a wish?

My eyes traced the rest of the verse that I had just copied. "They will be my people, and I will be their God, for they will return to me wholeheartedly."

The last word caused me to stop and press my lips together. *Wholeheartedly.* Did I love God wholeheartedly? Did I serve Him wholeheartedly?

I knew the answer, but I didn't speak it aloud or allow myself to ponder it. I didn't want to think about it right then. I never intended for this trip to turn into a spiritual retreat.

With polite and reverent motions, I closed the Bible and placed it in the bottom drawer with my T-shirts. Long ago I had learned that God's Word was quick, powerful, and sharper than any two-edged sword. I knew that was true. I just didn't feel ready to be sliced and diced. Not here. Not now.

Without saying it overtly, I told God that if He was thinking of doing a makeover on my heart, I wanted to wait until I returned home. While I was in England, I preferred that all the old furniture in my heart and mind stayed right where it was. That way I could come and go as I pleased, and even when the lights were turned off, I knew where everything was so I didn't bump into any of my issues.

I picked up the remote control and figured out how to turn on the television. Flipping through the channels, I found a fun chick flick I hadn't watched in a long time. Nothing like a light-hearted film to take my mind off anything I didn't want to think about.

"Kellie, you're not going to believe what's on TV." I fluffed the pillows on my bed, settled back, and transferred my focus to the movie.

The first commercial break caught me off guard. Everyone in the advertisement was speaking with a British accent. It felt strange to watch a familiar movie in which everyone spoke with an American accent, just as if I were watching the movie at home. Then came the commercials, and I remembered where I was.

Kellie emerged from the tub and enthusiastically joined me in watching the silly movie. We were on vacation, and we could watch whatever we wanted without any competition for the remote control.

The movie had a lulling effect on us, and we ended up going to bed early without eating dinner. We were too comfortable to go back out and almost too groggy to eat.

Both Kellie and I were awake before six the next morning. We were ready to eat then and took advantage of the free meal included with our reservation by ordering the complete English breakfast and asked to have it delivered via room service.

While we waited, I took my turn in the luxury bathtub and realized how rarely I set aside time to soak in the tub at home. True, my bathtub was nothing like this deluxe one, but that didn't matter. Being submerged in the warm water and surrounded by the vanilla and lavender scent of the provided bath gel was heavenly. I decided to make an effort once I returned home to enjoy a scented bath at least once a week, whether I thought I needed it or not. Showers had other powers and ministering benefits. But they weren't a substitute for a bath.

Our food arrived minutes after I emerged from the tub feeling like Queen Esther after one of her royal perfuming soaks. Now it was time to dine like a queen as well. A rolling table was set up for us between our two beds. The warming lids were lifted, and Kellie and I stared at more food than either of us thought we could eat. We did a thorough evaluation as we tried a little of everything in front of us.

The bacon was flat and wide and nothing like our crisp American version. The two fried eggs were less cooked than we were used to yet not runny. A small scoop of baked beans came on the plate alongside half a broiled tomato. Unusual by our breakfast standards, but all of it was delicious. We also had orange juice, tea, and a bowl of some sort of flake cereal with a pitcher of whole milk. We had so much food it didn't matter that the bread was more toasted than we would have preferred. Instead of eating the toast, we opted for devouring the small buns dotted with bits of orange. They came to us warm, and when we cut them open and spread the pale dairy butter over the spongy interior, it was like having dessert for breakfast.

"I can't eat another bite," Kellie said.

"I can't believe how many carbs we've devoured since we've been here. Not that I'm complaining, because I'm loving all the bread."

"Tomorrow I think I'm going to order the fruit and yogurt plate." Kellie pushed back from the table. "That was exceptionally delicious, though. What time do you think we should plan to leave here?"

"The sooner the better. We have a lot of ground to cover before we indulge in all this good stuff again at three o'clock at the Ritz."

"Don't you mean we have a lot of underground to cover?"

I smiled. She was starting the puns already this morning. It was going to be a good day.

We found our way to the tube station about twenty minutes later. The Holborn Station was located only a few blocks from our hotel.

I was amazed at how many people were out on the street on a weekday morning. Traffic was bumper to bumper, and it felt as if nearly that many bodies were moving up and down the street. We were a bit discombobulated because the pedestrians kept to the left side of the sidewalk while our inclination was to keep to the right.

"Did you see me crash into that poor guy?" Kellie asked as we stepped into the entrance of the tube station. "I guess they walk in the same direction they drive. I didn't see his turn signal."

"Are you sure he didn't try to pick your pocket?" I was conscious that we had moved out of the friendly countryside and were in the middle of a bustling metropolis. It was comparable to walking out of a scene from Jane Austen's lilting *Emma* and stepping into a Dickens street scene with David Copperfield on our heels.

Kellie did a quick check. Her passport and wallet were securely in place. "No, the collision was my fault."

After picking what looked like the shortest line, or queue, we stepped up to the machine against the wall and tried to figure out how to use it. The system looked similar to ATMs, and the instructions were clear. Kellie's debit card didn't work, so we used my Visa and purchased one-way tickets to the station closest to the Tower of London.

"We could probably save money with one of these other options," I said.

"We can figure out the details later. We have what we need for now."

Commuters in a much greater hurry than we were brushed by as we figured out how to put our small paper tickets through the machine that let us into the gate area. We followed the crowds and stepped onto the steepest escalator I've ever seen. The moving stairs in the well-lit area took us farther and farther down. Along the walls poster after poster advertised the current plays on in London.

"What do you think?" Kellie turned to look at me from the escalator step directly below mine.

"I think this is the opposite of yesterday when we were going up in the balloon. Now we're going down. Really down. Does this freak you out?"

"Not really. When I asked what you thought, I was referring to all these ads for the theater. I wanted to know which play you thought we should see."

"Oh. Any of them would be fine with me."

"I've always wanted to see *Les Misérables*," Kellie said. "What do you think?"

"*Oui, oui! Les Misérables* it is."

The escalator deposited us into a well-lit passageway where more steps led us down a tile-lined corridor and onto a landing. Dozens of people stood on the long stretch of cement. Across from the narrow area where the lowered tracks carried the subway cars was a curved wall covered with large advertisements for popular brands of clothing and perfume.

In a funny way I appreciated the billboards and the bright lights because it took away the sensation that we were standing deep beneath the city of London. I didn't have time to decide if that should make me uncomfortable, because our train arrived with a whoosh of air. Kellie and I pressed in with the other travelers.

No seats were available, so we stood and held on to the poles as the train pulled forward swiftly and smoothly.

Our airport in Orlando has a small monorail that transports passengers a short distance on an elevated track. It feels more like an amusement ride than a means of transportation. This subway gave me the feeling I was in a big city.

A map near the door showed the underground line we were on with each stop clearly marked. I liked looking at the faces of all the people seated and standing as we were spirited through the belly of London. The nationalities in our car were diverse. Some travelers were on their way to work. Others looked weary, as if they were headed home. Young students were easy to identify because of their uniforms. One woman wearing earphones leaned back and closed her eyes. The man beside her held a cell phone and seemed to be scrolling through his messages. His shirt was buttoned lopsided with two empty buttonholes at the neck. I wondered if he would discover his dressing error before he arrived at his destination.

Our exit from the tube was a repeat of our getting on, only in reverse. Another steep escalator lifted us back to street level where our tickets were once again inserted into an automatic gate.

When we were outside, we followed the signs to the Tower of London and were both awed at the size of the medieval fortress that sits on the river's edge. The tall stone wall that surrounds the tower was intimidating and more massive than we had expected.

"William the Conqueror began building this medieval fortress in..." Kellie paused, looking at one of the many travel brochures we had cherry-picked from the assortment available at our hotel. "Are you ready for this? Almost a thousand years ago. The year was 1078. Can you even begin to grasp that?"

"No. We just don't know what old is, do we?"

She read on. "Inside these eighteen acres the sovereigns of England have housed a prison, a palace, chapels, a museum, and an execution site."

"And the Crown Jewels, right?"

"Right. If we don't want to go on a tour, we can go directly to the Waterloo Barracks to see the Crown Jewels."

I liked the idea of being on our own time schedule, but Kellie was hesitant about our winging it. "I don't know," she said. "We won't have any information on what we're seeing. All we have is this brochure. We're going to miss a lot of interesting details if we don't go on a tour."

"Well, maybe they have short tours." I didn't want to be the impatient tourist since this spot was on Kellie's top-five list. I also knew that if she and I were going to end up having any squabbles on this trip, it would be over details like this. I liked having a glimpse of the big picture, finding my favorites of the moment, and then moving on. Kellie liked to pause and ponder.

I thought about how she could have lingered much longer when she found the Morris tapestry along with the Tolkien bust at Exeter Chapel. I had a feeling she picked up the pace and slid out when she did not only because of the organist stopping in midrehearsal but also because I was already out the door.

The solution, I decided, was for me to be sensitive to what would be most enjoyable for her, especially at the locales that were on her list and not on mine. An extra hour gazing at a rug or relic wouldn't kill me. This was London! The Tower of London, to be precise. I'd waited most of my life to come and see all this. So what was my hurry? It was time to stop and smell the history of this place.

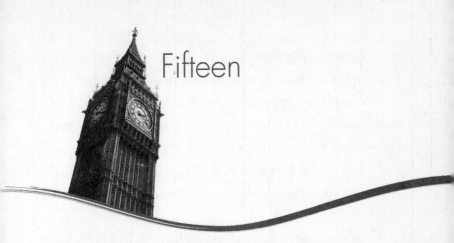

Fifteen

When we paid our admission fee for the Tower of London, we found we could rent portable recordings that corresponded with points of interest. If we wanted to pass up one part of the grounds but stop to view another, all we had to do was press the number that was posted on the marker of the site we were standing in front of. This was the kind of tour that made both of us happy.

Our first stop was on the fortress's waterside. We climbed up to the top of a walkway that allowed us to look out at the wide, murky River Thames and to take some fantastic photographs of the Tower Bridge. I thought we were looking at the famous London Bridge until another tourist with an American accent corrected me.

"The London Bridge is in Arizona," he said. "At Lake Havasu City. We've been there to see it. I heard the bridge was bought for two and a half million and was shipped over, stone by stone, because it was falling down from all the traffic here. The Tower Bridge you're looking at is much more interesting. Trust me."

We nodded our appreciation for his opinions and took a few more pictures of the impressive suspension bridge before the sun dipped behind an incoming army of clouds. The two towers on the bridge reminded me of gigantic chess pieces with their spires and turrets sticking up in the sky and threatening to puncture any cloud that came too close.

As we made our way to the Waterloo Barracks, four Beefeaters passed in front of us. We quickly pulled out our cameras to join many other tourists in the picture-taking fest. These traditional guards wore regal blue dress uniforms with bright red trim. On their heads were tall, black-brimmed hats circled with more red trim. Everyone stopped to watch them pass.

Next came two Beefeaters in the more elaborate traditional scarlet uniforms trimmed in gold with lots of emblems across the front of the uniforms, including a gold crown. Their black hats were much more impressive with red, white, and blue bows that gave the appearance of a halo of bright flowers. At their necks, intricately pleated lace stuck out like a white circular collar. They wore scarlet knee socks and black cobbler-style shoes. The pageantry of their appearance was stunning.

"Did you know that the lace used by royalty and probably for these royal guards was once made in Olney?" Kellie asked.

"What number are you listening to?" I held up my audio wand.

"That's not on the recorded tour. Don't you remember when Opal told us that Olney was a lace-making town? Or was it Rose? Anyway, it just seems interesting now to see a traditional costume and how much lace they used."

We kept walking, listening to the description of the various buildings on the large grounds.

"Did you listen to the explanation of why they're called Beefeaters?" Kellie asked.

I nodded. "Nice benefit working for royalty. You get to eat well."

"Right, but did you hear what the recording said about how the name *Beefeater* was a derogatory term?"

"I'm sure all the guards who weren't getting their share of the beef were the ones who started the nickname. They were jealous of the fat guys in the fancy uniforms, I would guess."

"And what was that part about the ravens?" Kellie asked as we stopped to look at a map. "Had you ever heard that before? The part about the ancient prophecy that as long as the ravens resided in the Tower of London, the kingdom wouldn't fall."

"No, I hadn't heard that before. I think it's kind of funny that to help fulfill the prophecy, eight ravens with clipped wings—to keep them from flying away—reside here. We can go see them if you want."

Kellie raised her chin like an eager child. "How about if we see the jewels first?"

"Diamonds before ravens. Fine with me."

We meandered through a museum of historic lore before entering a dark, high-security room where the royal crowns and scepter are kept under glass and guard. A slow-moving conveyor belt advances viewers past the dazzling display.

In front of us was a group of schoolchildren on a tour. My favorite moment was when three little princesses-in-the-making stood between the display and us. The girls in their blue school uniforms and pigtails drew in a collective "Oohhh!" as they viewed the crown that held a diamond nearly as large as one of their fists.

"Imagine that on your head," one of the little dreamers said.

"You would have to marry the prince to wear that," another said.

"Then I would be the queen."

"If you were the queen, you would have to live in Buckingham Palace."

"If I lived in Buckingham Palace, I'd have my own horse. And I would eat ice cream every day."

"If I were the queen," the third one said, "I would have a unicorn, and I would make a crown just like that one for my unicorn to wear."

"Me too. I would have two unicorns, if I were the queen."

Kellie and I smiled at each other as the schoolgirls stepped off the moving walkway and, joining hands, hurried to catch up with the rest of their group.

"Adorable," Kellie said. "I hope one of my married sons has a baby soon. I would love to have a granddaughter to spoil."

Was part of England's allure the marvel of the long-lasting monarchy? For young subjects with pigtails, a mystique as sweet as the dream of unicorns circled around the thought that they could grow up one day to be the queen of England.

We concluded the tour in the gift shop, where we bought a few postcards and then headed for the Beauchamp Tower. In this very old tower, prisoners who had nothing but time on their hands had etched a sort of medieval graffiti into the walls. Some simply carved their names. Others did elaborate carvings including crosses, their family coat of arms, dates, circumstances of their imprisonment, and even poems.

One of the names we lingered over was "Jane." We pressed the corresponding number on our audio tour and heard that this bold carving possibly was etched by the imprisoned husband of Lady Jane Grey. In 1553, at the age of sixteen, Lady Jane Grey was named successor to the throne only to be overthrown nine days later and beheaded.

The mysteries of the monarchy probably are lost on those of us who have known only democracy. But the tour made me consider how unique Great Britain is. Five hundred years ago a young woman could lose her head for being crowned queen, while today a young girl can dream of having the royal crown placed on her head.

Kellie and I put together our unaffected heads and studied the map. Our speedy, self-guided tour allowed us to see everything we were most interested in at the Tower of London and still leave us almost four hours before our three o'clock teatime at the Ritz.

"What do you think about going to Harrods next?" Kellie asked. "And maybe the Victoria and Albert Museum. They're not especially close to where we are now, but the underground is so fast I think we could get there and back to this side of town for the Ritz easily enough."

"We can give it a try. If we have to adjust along the way, we'll adjust."

"Ebb and Flo," Kellie said.

I nodded. "Ebb and Flo."

"I just want to make sure I'm not getting too bossy and only going after the sights that I added to the list. I want to make sure this is something you want to do as well."

I smiled. "You don't have to worry about me. I want to do and see everything while we're here."

I was still smiling when Kellie and I stepped into Harrods, the most elaborately decorated department store either of us had ever been in. The founder of Harrods was credited as once saying customers could buy anything from a "pin to an elephant." One brazen customer supposedly went to the pet department and asked to order an elephant. The response from the clerk was, "African or Indian? Male or female?"

I relayed that bit of trivia to Kellie as we entered the store, and she said, "I definitely don't want to buy an elephant. I wouldn't mind finding the ladies' washroom, though."

We found the immaculate facilities easily enough but weren't prepared for the pinkness of it all, nor did we understand the procedure of paying the maid for the use of the rest room. She wore a proper maid's uniform with an apron and offered us towels to dry our hands. On a corner end table was a china dish where we watched another customer deposit a few coins before putting aside her used towel.

"Call me pessimistic..." I said as we exited the rest room.

"You? Pessimistic? Never."

"I'm just thinking that if the rest of this retail theme park is anything like that bathroom, I won't be able to afford a pair of jeans here, and that was the one item I needed to shop for."

"Then do you mind if we start in the stationery department? I've been wanting a purse-sized notebook since I didn't bring one with me. I've wanted to take notes about so many things, and I'm afraid I've graffitied all your information pages."

"First stop, stationery." Taking a short escalator, we followed signs to the stationery department and browsed table after table of stacked leather-bound notebooks. We saw daily planner–style calendars advertised as "diaries" and lots of address books. I found a blank notebook I liked and willingly paid the high price because it was so nicely made. Kellie found another style for half the price and decided to buy it.

"Do you want to try looking for jeans?" Kellie asked after the journal was tucked into my shoulder bag.

"Not yet. Why don't we just keep exploring? This place is fascinating."

"I know. It's so organized."

I smiled. Leave it to Kellie to admire the organizational features of one of the world's most prestigious department stores.

We navigated our way through the store to an amazing food court that was nothing like any food court I had ever seen. This area was more like an archipelago of food stations, each different in personality and offerings. The food islands seemed to stay afloat in a sea of humans, all sniffing the air, looking right and left at the options. A feeding frenzy was about to take place.

I almost regretted that neither of us was hungry yet. It would have been fascinating to try some of the specialties prepared at the individual stations. We ambled along and ended up in an area devoted to tea, chocolate, and coffee.

The aroma was magnificent. An employee with a tray offered us samples of a specialty drinking chocolate that she said came from an ancient Aztec recipe. We sipped the treasured drink from tiny white paper cups and with wide-eyed agreement stood in line to buy a decorative tin of the chocolate pearls that she said would dissolve in hot water or hot milk.

I loved the carnival atmosphere in that department. It felt exotic, like a Mediterranean spice market. These goods had come from the four corners of the earth, and here they were, gathered in one well-stocked department, waiting for eager pilgrims to sample a taste. My theatrical thoughts might have had something to do with the Italian salami and provolone we had just sampled. Or it could be I was having one of those moments when I realized I wasn't in "Kansas anymore." We had nice stores in Florida but nothing like this all under one roof.

As Kellie paid for her chocolate, I lingered over the variety of teas in beautiful tins. One of the teas was named "Lady Grey," and I decided to buy it, thinking of Lady Jane Grey, whose name we had just seen carved in the Tower of London.

Kellie picked up a tin of Darjeeling tea, and I teased her, saying, "You're copying me. You're buying everything I'm buying."

"Well, Lady Flo, what can I say? You have good taste."

We made our way into the very fragrant fragrance department and were amazed at all the shoppers buzzing around the nectar hubs. It really felt as if we were removed from any sense of time of day as we wandered from one department to the next. Outside it could be rainy or sunny. It didn't matter. In here, all was alive with color and scent and a pervading sense of Victorian ornamental poshness.

I don't know if Kellie meant to take so much time at the shelf that was lined with boxed sets of fragrances and lotions, but she caught the eye of one of the salesclerks, who came over. The well-dressed woman described the benefits of a particular product and the added value of buying the promotional gift box.

"I really am only interested in buying the lotion," Kellie said.

I found the sample atomizer of the fragrance Kellie was considering and gave my wrist a spritz. "Kellie, you should get the set." I came alongside her and let her sniff my wrist. "It's a nice fragrance."

She hesitated.

"Do I need to buy one first so you'll copy me?"

I remembered what Martin had told me a few days before we left. He said my job on this trip was to make sure Kellie spent a little extra on herself. He was afraid she would hesitate over something she really liked and then would come home and regret she hadn't bought it when she had the chance.

With best-friend audacity, I said to the salesclerk, "She needs to buy the set. Don't let her get only the lotion. Keep telling her what a great deal it is."

Kellie laughed and gave in without further debate. I told her I had just done my job for the trip and Martin would be pleased. She had no idea what I was talking about. While she paid for the fragrance gift set, I peered at the makeup display.

"Are you going to buy something too?" Kellie asked.

"Of course. We're having a contest, or didn't you know? You're two items ahead of me."

The salesclerk tilted her head and looked at me from under the long lashes of her perfectly made-up eyes. "Have you considered using an eyebrow pencil?"

"I do sometimes." I automatically touched my brows. "I know my eyebrows are fading away, but I don't like them to be too dark."

"We have a lovely pencil in a soft brown that comes with a smudger. I think it would work nicely for you."

"A smudger?"

She showed me the sample item with the soft tip at one end and the retractable eyeliner pencil on the other. "This allows you to blend the color and make it more natural. Would you like me to demonstrate on you?"

"Do you mean have our makeup done?" Kellie asked.

"If you like, yes, my assistant and I would be glad to do that for both of you."

Kellie looked excited. I knew she loved this sort of thing but rarely allotted time or money for such extras. While she had spent the last fifteen years driving her three sons to football practice, doing their mounds of laundry, and launching them out of the house, I was getting my fill of teenage-daughter times, indulging in long makeup sessions and toenail-painting evenings. Kellie missed out on all that. This would be a nice treat for her.

"We're going to tea at the Ritz." Kellie took a seat on the high stool. "We have to be there at three. But we wanted to have a quick tour of the V and A since it's so close."

"Lovely," the makeup artist said. "We have plenty of time to get the two of you looking your best for your afternoon events. Do you have plans for the evening as well?"

Kellie leaned over and touched my arm. "I think tonight is the night we should go to the theater. *Les Misérables.*"

"Why not?"

"We can arrange the tickets for you here in guest services, if you like," the cosmetician said.

Once again my answer was, "Why not?"

"I'll make a quick call and be right back."

From there on, Kellie and I were sitting ducks. But I must say, we were the most content of all sitting ducks because it had been a long, long time since either of us had been so pampered. Besides, it was easy to comply. The London Princess Syndrome was taking effect on me. I supposed if I had to sit in the cushy chair and have my makeup done at Harrods, then I would. And if we had to go to tea at the Ritz, so be it. Such are the obligations when you take on the role of princess for the day.

Sixteen

Kellie made a glorious discovery at the Victoria and Albert Museum when she asked at the desk if any William Morris items were open for viewing.

"There is an entire room, the Morris room, that he decorated," Kellie reported to me, her cheeks flushed with excitement. "It's at the back on the ground floor. I want to go there first. I also found out they have a chair and a chest he designed. Those are upstairs."

"Lead on."

We wound our way through an elaborate display of women's dresses from the past several centuries. Many of the garments we looked at through the glass cases were original dresses. I thought they were fascinating, especially because of the way they showed the changes in styles over the years.

But Kellie thought the Morris room was breathtaking. I stood beside her and gazed at the warm harmony of greens, blues, and golds. The style was beginning to look familiar. Nature's bounty of vines, birds, and leaves seemed to be the foundational theme in the elaborate work that covered the walls. But interjected into that overall sense of nature were beautiful paintings of women in flowing gowns with untamed hair and faraway expressions, as if an ethereal world of classic Greek statues had posed for the paintings.

"Think of the typical Victorian décor," Kellie said. "Heavy tapestries, fringed cloth, ornately carved furniture, lots of bric-a-brac…"

I nodded. I knew exactly what she meant.

"Into the decorating world, Morris and his Pre-Raphaelite brothers introduced these fresh colors and simplicity. They brought the natural world back inside with their wallpaper and tapestry designs that were in harmony with nature, yet they added this romantic dash of medieval mystery. Think of King Arthur and the Knights of the Round Table."

She pulled out her camera and asked me to take a photo of her in front of the vine relief wall next to an inset painting of one of the captivating, stately women in a flowing gown. Several visitors were seated at a table nearby, sipping tea that could be purchased along with other snacks from the lunchroom located next to the Morris room.

"Would you both like to be in the photo?" a bald man asked us. His accent was French.

"Sure. Thanks."

Kellie and I stood close and grinned broadly with our lovely makeup giving us a boost in camera confidence, I think. We meandered through the room, taking a few more pictures before dashing to the other end of the museum to view more original Morris designs. This display included handmade chairs and an amazing chest painted by Morris with scenes from the legend of George and the Dragon. The colors were black with dark orange and warm brown shades. The depth and dimension drew me to the figures.

If we hadn't been in such a fury to get to our tea date on time, I'm sure we would have lingered at the museum until it closed. I loved hearing Kellie's hidden knowledge of decorating styles and seeing her passion for art and color.

A ready taxi with its trademark spacious backseat transported Kellie and me and all our shopping bags to the front entry of the Ritz Hotel. The entrance wasn't nearly as dramatic as the front of our hotel, but once we stepped inside, we were taken in with the charm of this five-star hotel. We checked our shopping bags and coats and took a minute to freshen up in the rest room, which had a definite French feel to it as well as another towel-offering chambermaid with her tip dish.

Approaching the Palm Court inside the lobby where the afternoon tea was served, Kellie and I lowered our voices, took inventory of our outfits, and fretted over not being as up to code as we should have been. I had on my only pair of pants, which were a dressy, dark brown, with a cream-colored cable-knit sweater and a long-sleeved T-shirt underneath. The sweater made the outfit lean toward the casual side; yet I was afraid that if I stripped down to the plain white T-shirt, I would look more like an over-the-hill soccer mom than my desired identity of Lady Flo of the Palm Court Tea Room.

"Kellie, I need nicer clothes," I whispered.

She looked much more suited for her role as Lady Ebb. I hoped the hostess would let me in since I was with the well-dressed woman in the black pants and pressed, royal blue, long-sleeved blouse. Kellie's silver necklace and earrings helped to pull off a more polished look than my turquoise clip-on earrings that didn't exactly match anything. I truly did own nice outfits. But when it came to winter wear, I was limited.

"You look great, Liz. The dress code is no jeans or tennis shoes, so you and I are just fine."

"Then it's a good thing Opal isn't with us wearing her hot pink tennies!"

"I've been thinking about Opal and Rose today too. I wonder how they're getting along."

"I wonder how Opal and Virgil are getting along," I said with a grin.

"Do you really think there was something between them?"

"Yes, definitely. Love knows no limits. Not even age or testy twin sisters."

"Do you think we should call them just to check in?" Kellie asked.

"That would be a good idea. Should we try calling tonight before the play?"

"Sure."

By the time we were seated in the padded chairs at a round table with a smoothly pressed tablecloth on it, I wasn't thinking about Opal and Virgil or my appearance any longer. The Palm Court itself was the best dressed in the house. Next to her marble pillars, explosive, golden, glowing chandeliers, and exultant palm ferns that stretched to the elevated glass ceiling, all of us were underdressed. The buttery seashell color of the walls worked perfectly with the soft light from the sconces and chandeliers and the natural light coming through the spider-web design on the glass ceiling. In the center of the main wall was an alcove, complete with a life-size statue of a golden woman reclining by a fountain. Who could compete with any of that?

We ordered the Ritz traditional English tea to accompany our very expensive but very sumptuous selection of sandwiches and pastries. Our efficient middle-aged waiter in his dark suit and bow tie seemed to take great pride in describing for us the variety of sweets on the sterling silver tiered tray.

The orderly British mind-set was at work with the presentation of our afternoon tea. The items were appropriately grouped. If we chose to start on the lowest level of the three tiers, we could work our way from the sandwiches up to the scones on the second level and finish with the sweets on the top level.

With masterful motions of his hand, our server pointed out each of the treats. "Your assortment of tea sandwiches includes smoked salmon, egg mayonnaise with watercress, ham, chicken with mayonnaise, and the traditional cucumber with dairy butter."

The perfectly cut, crustless sandwich squares were lined up on their sides, making it easier to see the layers as he described them. Even the sandwiches were better dressed than Kellie or I.

"It's a good thing they're so small," Kellie said in a low voice.

I nodded but already was eying the scones on the second tier.

"Here we have our freshly baked raisin and apple scones with Devonshire clotted cream and organic strawberry preserves," he said.

"May I ask," Kellie turned her chin up to the waiter, unintentionally interrupting him, "do we put the clotted cream on the scone first or the strawberry jam?"

Without a change in expression, he stated, "The choice is entirely yours, madam. Many of our guests enjoy the cream first and then the preserves."

"Thank you." Kellie gave me a silly side grimace, as if she had been caught passing notes in class during the lecture.

"To conclude," our expert waiter said with a sweeping gesture at the top tier, "you will find an assortment of our pastries and cakes here. The fruits of the forest compote with English cream is one of our specialties. Now, have you any questions?"

Neither of us could think of anything intelligent to ask.

"If there are no questions, may I pour your tea?"

"Yes, please," we said in Lady-Ebb-and-Lady-Flo unison.

With my hands folded in my lap, I pushed my shoulders back in an effort to sit up straighter. The elegance of the Palm Court had that effect. The fragrant amber liquid came steaming out of the sterling silver teapot's spout into the delicate china cup in front of me. The waiter used a silver strainer as he poured the tea. Only a few squiggly black tea leaves were caught by the strainer, which was then placed in its own silver nest until it would be called on to strain my refill.

Being served so expertly by a uniformed waiter felt like another form of pampering. As soon as he stepped away, I told Kellie I didn't know how much more of this extravagance I could take.

"This is pretty over the top, isn't it?" She picked up the intricately decorated silver tongs and reached for one of the cucumber sandwiches. "It's amazing how the décor of a room can affect how you feel about yourself and your surroundings. Maybe that's why I love decorating so much. I love elevating people's environment so that it elevates their feelings about themselves."

"Sounds like the princess mentality again."

"Yes, but in a good way. In a way that makes you remember that you are fearfully and wonderfully made. That's what God says of us. I think we suppress our appreciation for the 'wonderfully made' part far too often."

"We have so much," I said. "While we were in Harrods, I was thinking we are so, so blessed. Both of us have husbands who are at a place in their careers where they are able to provide everything we need as well as a good amount of what we want. Do you realize how many women would love to be in our situations?"

"Yes, I do."

"It's almost an embarrassment of riches."

With a calm expression, Kellie leaned over. "We are extravagantly, incredibly blessed. This is a rare abundance. It is. But it wasn't always this way for either of us."

"You're right."

"I don't think we should be embarrassed about the goodness in this season of life simply because it seems so extravagant. Our heavenly Father is extravagant with His children sometimes. He gave us this trip. He's provided all of this. I think we can honor Him best by receiving these gifts and letting ourselves overflow with gratefulness."

"I'm beyond grateful at this point," I said. "I'm in awe. Amazed. It's just so much grace. So much goodness."

"And don't you think it delights our heavenly Father to pour out such an 'amazing grace' gift on two of His princess daughters?"

I took another sip of tea, and together we quietly made our way through the savories and sweets on the silver-tiered tea tray.

"The way I see it," Kellie said, "this whole trip is a gift in much the same way that you made the reservations for us to have tea here and said it was my birthday gift. What if I said, 'No, it's too much. I only gave you a card and a pedicure for your birthday last year. I can't enjoy this because it's too extravagant, and it's more than I could return in a gift to you for your birthday next year'?"

Kellie sipped her tea, poured in a little milk, and took another sip before concluding her thought. "I think God is best honored and pleased when we simply receive His abundant gifts."

I nodded and tucked another nibble of the egg sandwich into my mouth.

A pianist had been filling the open room with lovely music since we had arrived. In the stretch of quiet between Kellie and me, my ears tuned in to the melodic chords, and I sat back to listen.

At the table next to us an elderly woman in a blue silk sari spoke a language I had never heard. Across from us I picked up a few—very few—French words from two young women in stylish business suits. They were much more invested in their conversation than they were in the barely touched food on their tiered tray.

I replayed some of Kellie's comments in my mind. Could it sometimes be as easy as that with God? Does He merely want us to receive His goodness and be thankful? The verse I had read from Jeremiah lilted over my thoughts lightly, like the chords on the piano in the background: "I will give them hearts that will recognize me as the LORD. They will be my people, and I will be their God, for they will return to me wholeheartedly."

I wondered if being grateful in seasons and in moments like this was part of what happens when a heart is bent toward recognizing that God is the Lord of all. He gives, and He takes away. Today He was giving. A lot.

"You have to try one of these." Kellie took another dainty bite of a gorgeous berry tart in a flaky pastry shell.

The berry tart dissolved slowly on my tongue. I sipped just enough cream-laced tea to let the sweet and tart sensation linger on my taste buds. In an odd little private ceremony, I closed my eyes and thought, *You provided all this, Father God. My heart recognizes Your abundant goodness in this, and I receive it with deep and humble thanks.*

The rest of the afternoon and evening I moved around inside a quietness of my spirit. We decided to walk part of the way back to our hotel where we planned to leave our shopping bags before going to the theater at seven. It felt good to stretch our legs after all the delicious tea treats we had eaten.

For such an unassuming collection of dainty, one-bite foods, both Kellie and I couldn't believe how full we felt.

"I think something happens in one's stomach when the tea mixes with the pastry flour," Kellie said. "I think it all expands."

I smiled.

"Don't you feel like we ate twice as much as we really did?"

"At least twice," I agreed. "Maybe three times as much."

Neither of us wanted any dinner before the play. We freshened up and took a taxi to the theater district, thinking we had allowed plenty of time. However, the cab bogged down in an area where the streets were narrow. So many people were walking on either side of the sidewalk that it appeared to be a march, with everyone moving as one.

"We must be near the theater district." Kellie pulled out our tickets and checked the name of the theater. She leaned forward to get the driver's attention. "Is the Queen's Theatre within walking distance?"

He rattled off the directions, and we made the decision to pay him and hoof it the rest of the way. Our cab seemed to be at the epicenter of the vehicle bottleneck.

I paid the fare this time. It was all part of our Lady-Ebb-and-Lady-Flo system. Kellie had paid for the fare last time.

We were pressed on both sides as we walked through the crowd. Nearly all the major theaters are located in the same area, near Leicester Square. Anyone who wants to see a major production comes to this area, which makes walking a better alternative than paying to sit in a taxi.

Three blocks down we saw the Queen's Theatre. Large, permanent signs on the side of the building declared that this production had been running continuously for more than a decade. Kellie and I jostled our way through the throngs of people, found the correct line, and took our place in the orderly queue in front of the theater.

"That was easy," she said.

I laughed. We apparently had differing ideas on the meaning of *easy.*

We entered the theater with a crush of people and decided to leave our jackets at the coat check. A uniformed usher pointed out our seats, and we made our way down the slanted aisle toward the front of the theater. Both of us grinned as soon as we sat down. These were good seats. We were midway back on the lower level and at the perfect spot in the slope of the theater to see over the heads in front of us.

The seat next to me was empty, and I hoped no one claimed it. I liked crossing my legs in the narrow space and stretching out my elbow on the armrest.

A sense of anticipation flitted through the theater. I hadn't been to a play in a long time. The expectation here was so different from the laid-back feeling in a movie theater. I couldn't picture anyone here putting his feet on the back of the seat in front of him. No one would slurp a giant-sized soft drink or drop popcorn from a jumbo tub onto this floor.

We were definitely at the theater London-style. A couple dressed in formal attire took their seats several rows in front of us. The house lights flicked off and on. Conversations rose to a louder buzz and then softened as the lights dimmed.

The performance was about to begin.

Seventeen

As soon as I crossed my legs and made use of the extra space in front of the vacant seat beside me, a gentleman in a sweater and tie shuffled his way through the dark and settled in the seat next to me.

"Almost didn't make it," he murmured, as if trying to make friendly conversation.

I didn't respond kindly to the late arriver. I just uncrossed my legs and shifted in my seat, miffed that my extra space was being claimed by its rightful owner.

The curtain rose. Having never seen *Les Misérables* before, I wasn't prepared for what happened in the first scene when Jean Valjean was caught with the stolen candlesticks. Nor was I prepared for the act of mercy demonstrated by the priest. His response to injustice wasn't normal or natural.

Watching mercy demonstrated on the stage touched something deep inside me, and I teared up to see extravagant love shown to someone who didn't deserve it. I dabbed at my tears and gave myself back over to the production. I don't think I moved once in my seat during the first and second acts. I was riveted.

Intermission came too soon. I didn't want to move. I wanted the actors to come back on stage and finish the story. "This is so powerful."

"It's fantastic. Do you know how it ends?" Kellie stood up to stretch.

"No. I've not seen it before."

"Ladies?" The gentleman beside me leaned into our conversation. "May I bring back something for either of you from the concessions?"

"No, thanks," Kellie answered for both of us.

"Great performance, isn't it?" His accent wasn't the same as the London accents we were becoming accustomed to. My guess was he was Irish, but I can't say why it seemed that way.

"Yes," Kellie answered. "The leads are doing an exceptional job."

"My daughter is an understudy for Fantine," he said proudly.

"She is? Is she performing tonight?" Kellie asked.

"No, she's been with the cast for three months and hasn't been on stage yet. She wouldn't give up her place, though. She loves the theater."

I spoke up. "I have a daughter who loves acting as well."

"Is she here in London?"

"No, she's in Florida."

"We're just here for a few days," Kellie said.

"I'm on a brief holiday as well. I've been promising my daughter for three months that I would come to see this production, and I'm finally making good on my word. I almost didn't make it, with the traffic and all."

In that short intermission chat, the gentleman beside me went from being a nuisance to a real person with common ground and reasons for me to feel connected to him. I hoped I could always remember how quickly my perspective of him changed once I had heard a little of his story.

Intermission ended. The curtain went back up, and we were all drawn into the performance again. During the final act of the play, the actor playing Jean Valjean knelt on the stage and offered up a piercing, feel-it-in-your-heart song entitled "Bring Him Home."

I blinked as the tears came again. This time I knew I wasn't alone. Kellie quietly sniffed. The man beside me gripped the armrest. All three of us seemed to hold our breath as the last note was released and left to hang in the air just above our heads.

The audience exploded with stunned applause. The man beside me sprang to his feet and bellowed, "Jesus Christ!" Across the auditorium other people rose in a standing ovation for the performer.

I was shocked at my neighbor's reaction. The man wasn't calling on the Lord's name in response to the actor's sung prayer. Yet he wasn't calling out the actor's name to praise him or yelling "bravo" either. Apparently he needed something powerful to shout in response to the beauty he had just experienced, so he shouted the name of Christ. I had never seen anyone do that before, and I was stunned by it.

The final act of the play continued, but I kept thinking of the prayer sung by Jean Valjean. All that his father-heart longed for was that Marius would return home safe and well after the battle.

The performance's impact came at me on a number of levels. As I stood with the rest of the audience at the curtain, applauding until my hands were sore, I hoped I would be able to hold on to all the impressions flooding me at that moment.

Kellie and I didn't talk much in the cab on the way back to our hotel. We entered our comfortable room, stretched out on our waiting beds, and stared at the ceiling as if watching a curtain call in our imaginations.

"That was amazing! Absolutely amazing. What a performance," Kellie said. "I've never seen anything like that. I didn't know the play had such a message of grace, did you?"

"No." I turned to her. "Did you see the man next to me after the 'Bring Him Home' song?"

"Yes. And do you know what it made me think? His reaction made me think of that verse that says every knee will bow and every tongue confess that Jesus Christ is Lord. Where is that verse? Philippians?"

"I think so. You know, after our tour of the Tower of London this morning, I have a stronger image of the power and glory associated with royalty. It's easier to imagine what it would be like to bow in front of the Sovereign Ruler."

"England, at least at one time, certainly had a grasp on what it was like to honor the Lord as the glorious King and majestic Ruler of all," Kellie said. "At least that's the impression I've been getting from some of the churches we've visited."

"And yet He's also our Father. His heart seems to always be turned toward His children, forever longing that each of them will 'come home' at the end of the long battle."

"Like Jean Valjean's solo," Kellie said.

"Exactly."

I fell asleep that night feeling close to my heavenly Father. In this great leap we had taken by flying to England, I had found that we weren't capriciously floating through the clouds when nothing was going according to schedule. We were truly held close in everlasting arms. So close, I felt as if I were beginning to hear God's heartbeat. Each measured beat was one of grace followed by an echo of love.

That night my dreams were sweetly serene. I woke feeling secure.

In the morning Kellie and I put our heads together and came up with a rip-roaring plan. At eight o'clock, dressed and with a satisfying breakfast of fruit, yogurt, and croissants in our bellies, we repeated our steps from the previous morning and went to the tube station. The underground took us back to Paddington Station, where we bought tickets for the half-hour ride to Windsor Castle.

We had decided on Windsor because the weather report that had been slipped under our door the night before promised sunshine. In some ways it seemed crazy to leave London when we still had so much to see in town. But after our taste of all things royal the day before, we both wanted to view Windsor Castle. It was the only must-see that appeared on both our lists. This was the day to go.

Standing on the platform at Paddington, waiting for train number five to pull in, Kellie and I sipped some hot tea in what the vendor at the kiosk called "takeaway" cups. I smiled, remembering the "Go Away" doormat at Rose's cottage.

"We forgot to call Rose and Opal last night before we went to the play," I said.

"You're right. We'll see them in just a few days. Maybe it's best not to call. If we do, they will probably try to convince us to return to Olney sooner than we planned."

"Good point." I drained my tea and looked across the train platform to a bench on track four where two children were sitting close, waiting for the train and swinging their legs. "You know what those two remind me of?"

"Paddington Bear?"

"No. The Pevensie children."

"Who are they?"

"Peter, Susan, Edmund, and Lucy. From Lewis's The Chronicles of Narnia. Do you remember how they were waiting at a train station and suddenly were transported to Narnia?"

Kellie nodded her recognition of what I was talking about.

I wondered for a whimsical moment if perhaps Lewis had once stood here on this very railway platform and imagined the opening scene of *Prince Caspian*. I looked around the train station, imagining what a creative mind like Lewis's would see in a place like this, just as I had pondered the Anglo-Saxon-looking Christ in the stained-glass window of Lewis's church and how that figure reminded me of Prince Caspian.

"Liz, how do you remember all those details from stories?"

"I don't know. They're just with me. I think I took them in during a time when my heart and mind were vulnerable and impressionable. They stayed with me."

"It's like you have a buried treasure," Kellie said. "I love the way you pull out these gems. Keep 'em coming!"

"I think that is my long-term passion: British literature. Particularly children's literature."

"You know, last night after the play I was thinking about passion. So many of the characters took risks and did what they were passionate about." Kellie tossed her paper cup into a rubbish bin a few feet away. "I want to do that."

"Do what?"

"I want to move forward with the decorating business. And I really would love for you to jump into this venture with me, Liz. I love the idea of the business being K & L Interiors. You and I make a good team."

I had to nod because I agreed with the part about making a

good team. But while Kellie had become more convinced about moving forward with her interior-design business, I had become more convinced I didn't want to enter into business with her. At least not as a partner.

Before I could respond, a young woman wearing an attractive, swishy skirt approached Kellie and me with a shy expression. "The train?" She pointed to the vacant space in front of us.

"We're waiting for the train to Windsor Castle," I said.

"It should be here in about three minutes," Kellie added.

"Good." She smiled.

"Are you going to Windsor Castle too?" I asked.

"Yes."

"Are you by yourself?"

She tilted her head like a curious bird and looked as if she hadn't understood my question. I guessed she was a tourist. She seemed to be in her early twenties and reminded me of my younger daughter.

"Is someone traveling with you?" I asked.

"No. *Moi*. Me only."

"Are you on vacation?" Kellie asked.

"Yes, I'm on my holiday." She grinned. "Sorry, my English is not so—"

"You're doing great," I told her.

The train pulled in right on time. The three of us stood back as the passengers disembarked.

"You're welcome to sit with us," Kellie said. "If you want to, that is."

The timid young woman gave us a grateful smile. "Yes. Thank you."

We found seats that faced each other, and for the next half hour, Kellie and I enjoyed getting to know Annette, who recently had graduated with an art degree from a university in southern France. With our very limited French and Annette's expansive English, we kept the conversation going.

When we arrived at the train station, we invited Annette to stay with us if she wanted to. And she did.

We walked up a well-worn cobbled road as Annette tried to formulate her questions, politely inquiring about our holiday and what we had enjoyed so far. She was most intrigued by our stories about the hot-air balloon ride.

We were puffing our way alongside lithe Annette as the road to the castle continued at a steady incline. The sky was a brilliant shade of fresh spring blue, and before us Windsor Castle rose with jaw-dropping majesty. The majesty wasn't due just to the sheer size and solid presence of the castle and surrounding grounds. Being on a hill, Windsor majestically commands a determined effort from those who want to come in her gates and participate in one of the tours.

Kellie, Annette, and I formed a jolly, rosy-cheeked trio by the time we made it to the ticket booth at the grounds' entrance.

Once again we opted for the self-guided tour that came with the audio wands. This was especially good for Annette because she could rent the French version.

Our tour began in a room that contained a fabulous doll-house built for Princess Anne. The three-story dollhouse came complete with miniature furniture in every room and working electric lights.

The royal family still occupies a portion of Windsor Castle. When I heard that, I assumed our tour would be limited. It wasn't. We walked through dozens of rooms, viewed endless pieces of original furniture, and lingered by the windows in one of the grand rooms where we could gaze out at the gardens and the peaceful-looking town that gathers at the hem of the sloping green castle grounds. We viewed cases filled with weapons, armor, and bits and pieces of historic memorabilia.

"What do you think?" I asked Annette. "Is this as much of a fairy-tale castle as castles in France?"

"I have only been to the Palace of Versailles. This castle I like more."

"Why?" I asked.

She seemed to have difficulty forming her sentence in response. "Versailles is a sad beauty to me. Much, much rich. Much of this." She pointed to one of the huge oil portraits in the hall.

"Too many portraits at Versailles?" I asked.

She didn't seem to recognize the word *portraits*.

"Paintings," Kellie tried. "Pictures of people. Are you saying the castle in France has too many pictures of famous people?"

"No, this." She pointed more directly at the highly detailed, inlaid gold carvings in the frame of one of the pictures.

"Ah! Too many ornate decorations. Too many fancy details in the décor."

"Yes, décor. Here, I like the beauty because it is a strong beauty. I like this castle."

"I like it too," I said. I also liked Annette's term "strong beauty."

All of us were ready at the same time to be done with the royal tour. We turned in our audio wands and exited the castle just as a procession was coming across the cobblestones. The three of us stood back to watch as the castle guards came marching by in stiff formation. The procession of the guards in their tall, bearskin hats and shiny brass-buttoned uniforms was powerful and impressive. We watched for more than ten minutes as the company moved into formation, shifted their bayonet-tipped weapons from one shoulder to the other, and clicked the heels of their well-shined boots. This was protocol to the smallest detail, and we were certain the drill was unfolding just the way it had been performed for centuries.

After a pleasant detour through the garden, where we took lots of pictures, Annette, Kellie, and I headed down the hill into town in search of some lunch. At one of the checkpoints along the stone wall, a castle guard stood like a statue in front of a small wooden guard station. He kept his gaze straight ahead from under the huge, rounded hat. His mannequin stance just begged us to go up to him and try to make him smile.

"Go ahead," I told Annette. "I'll take your picture."

She smiled, her shyness returning. "You first. I will take your picture."

"Okay." I took her challenge as if I were her twenty-two-year-old traveling companion and not someone who was almost old enough to be her grandmother.

Marching right up to the soldier, I stood as close as I dared and smiled nice and bright. The guard didn't flinch.

"Thank you," I said to him.

He didn't answer.

I walked back to where Kellie and Annette stood. "Your turn," I told Annette.

She grinned and tried to express her teasing suggestion. "I will make with the computer, the photo with my face on you."

"Oh no you won't! I stood by the guard. Now it's your turn."

"Go ahead." Kellie held out her hand and offered to take Annette's camera from her. "I'll take the picture."

"No, no, no." Annette shook her head.

"Oui, oui, oui," I said.

She laughed, pressed her shoulders back, and handed her camera to Kellie. "I have to be nice."

We weren't sure if that meant she was showing respect to the elderly, meaning Kellie and me, or if she was telling herself to be nice to the guard.

"Closer." Kellie looked through the viewfinder of Annette's camera. Annette was standing at least six feet away from the guard. I had stood only inches from him.

"Closer," I echoed.

Annette complied and made an adorably cute grimace. Kellie snapped the shot. The guard never flinched or gave any indication he was aware of our presence.

Annette joined us and in a coy voice said, "I think he wants to marry me."

We giggled together, and I thought of what a common denominator humor can be. Women around the world love to tease each other. Regardless of cultural differences or language barriers, women always can share a giggle over boys. Such is the evidence of an uncomplicated friendship.

In that spirit of uncomplicated camaraderie, we continued our chummy procession down the hill, settled gladly on the first tea shop we came to, and took a table by the front window. The shop was old, as evidenced by the uneven window frame that looked like a victim of centuries of settling.

"Did you see this quote on the menu about tea?" Kellie pointed to a line at the bottom. "It says, 'The cup that cheers but does not inebriate. William Cowper.'"

"Clever."

"Do you know what is this?" Annette pointed to an entry on the menu that was labeled "Teatime." At this simple yet very old tea shop, the "teatime" fare was nothing like the abundance served at the Ritz. Here it was two scones with clotted cream and jam along with a pot of tea.

I explained the "teatime" selection to Annette, and she closed her menu saying, "Yes. I have not eaten this."

"You haven't had scones and tea yet?" Kellie asked.

"No."

Kellie and I exchanged smiles. It felt fun being the ones to introduce sweet Annette to what might gladly become our new afternoon habit. Our smug thoughts were laughable because the two of us were far from experienced in matters of tea or scones or clotted cream.

Regardless, we both were looking pretty confident when the waitress came to our table and we placed the order for Annette. That's when I realized that Kellie and I suddenly had taken on the roles of Opal and Rose. We were the older women inviting the younger woman to be our travel companion. At least we hadn't asked Annette to carry anything for us yet, like folding spectator chairs.

But then, the day wasn't over.

Eighteen

"Where did the sunshine go?" Kellie asked, as we exited the tea shop at the foot of Windsor Castle.

The three of us looked up and gave a scowl to the gathering clouds. Over the last few days we had become so used to glorious sunshine and pristine blue skies that we almost had forgotten this was the onset of spring, and we were visiting a place that is notoriously green for a reason.

Our quick-footed trot the rest of the way down the hill to the train station was a feeble attempt to beat the coming raindrops. The raindrops won. We were damp when we boarded the train that would take us back to London, but the heater was going, and we dried out quickly.

On the ride back we exchanged our contact information with Annette and invited her to stay with us if she ever visited the Orlando area. She responded with the same kindness, saying, "You would be good for my mother. She does not go out of our small town. I wish her...she...I wish she be with me today."

We told her that until this trip, neither of us had gone anywhere adventurous without our husbands or families.

"When I told my daughter that Kellie and I were coming to England, she said we were going on a 'Sisterchicks' trip."

"'Sisterchicks'?"

"Like a girlfriends' getaway or a best friends' adventure. Maybe you and your mother can take a Sisterchicks trip and the two of you can visit us in Orlando."

"Maybe." Annette smiled. "It would be more possible that you would come to see us in France."

Our train rolled into Paddington Station, and the time came to say good-bye to Annette. I felt a sweet sadness. Annette seemed to feel it as well. She hugged me good-bye, pressing her cheek to mine and releasing a soft kiss into the air. She hugged Kellie the same way.

In a final tease I said, "In the movies they show the French people giving kisses on both cheeks."

Annette grinned and wagged a finger at me. "That is for only the French. You—you have only one kiss this time."

"Oh, I see how it is," I said, still teasing. "When Kellie and I come to France someday, maybe you can make us honorary Frenchwomen. Then, when we leave, you can give us two kisses."

"Or maybe three." She grinned as if she knew a few secrets

about French protocol that I wouldn't be able to decode on a single visit.

Annette left with a final wave, and Kellie and I looked at each other as if we had just lost our favorite kitten.

"She was a doll," I said.

"I hope she comes to Florida one day. Wouldn't that be fun?"

I nodded. "So? What do you think? Are we still planning to go from here to Buckingham Palace?"

"If you would like, sure. We're too late for the changing of the guard, but then we did see the drill with the castle guards."

"And it is raining," I added.

"What if we took a bus ride around town? We could go past Buckingham and get off if we want or keep riding if we want."

"Great idea, Kellie."

We found a bus stop right away and ducked under the covering with a dozen other people. Kellie read over the route information posted, and together we compared the posted route map with our foldout map. I'm sure our discussion made it obvious we were confused tourists, unsure which bus to take.

A young man dressed in a business suit and wearing a turban stood beside us and was privy to our conversations about Buckingham Palace and the other sights we were trying to see in one big loop.

"Madams, may I kindly give a recommendation?" His rich Indian accent reminded me of Sara Crewe's benevolent Ram Dass from Frances Hodgson Burnett's novel *A Little Princess*. As alluded to in the novel, Britain's influence in India at the turn of the nineteenth century caused a rapid increase in the Indian population in London. In crowded public places around London, such as the train stations, we had seen a much greater mix of cultures than we ever saw at home in Winter Park.

"If you take this one"—he pointed to one of the routes on the list—"bus 73 on the Green Line will take you past Hyde Park and Buckingham Palace. You can change at Victoria to whatever direction you need to go from there."

"Thank you," I said.

"You are most kindly welcome."

The next bus was packed with people who smashed their way into the limited standing space. Kellie and I pressed our way to the narrow metal stairs that led to the top level. Up top on the full double-decker bus, we found an open seat for the two of us along the right side toward the front. We bobbed along with fogged-up windows, trying to make out the sights below us.

One tourist tip I remembered reading at home the week before was to be sure to sit above the street level on a double-decker bus and not to always take the underground or a cab to travel about town. The reasoning was that, from this second-story perch, one would have an eye-level view of the intricate decorations on many of the Victorian buildings. This was the case as the bus plodded through the traffic before turning onto a main thoroughfare marked "Bayswater."

"We never finished our conversation," Kellie said.

"Which conversation was that?"

"This morning at the train station on our way to Windsor I was saying that I've decided I want to start the interior-design business. And I would love for you to be part of that with me. What do you think?"

"I…"

"I know it's not been the best time to think about it with everything else we've been doing."

"My mind has been a little occupied for the past week—"

"Yet I was hoping you might have an initial gut reaction to the idea."

The truth was, I did have a gut reaction, but I didn't want to tell Kellie yet. Not here. Not now.

While I had been facing Kellie, I had been stealing glances out the window and was aware that we had been following the rim of Hyde Park for many blocks. She was missing the great view of the immense greenery through the misting rain. I knew this was the park J. M. Barrie frequented as he was creating his stories of Peter Pan, but that didn't seem like a relevant point to add to our present conversation.

"You know what, Kellie?" I said as diplomatically as I could. "I think it would be easier for me if we picked up this conversation at another time."

"Okay. Sure. That makes sense. This is a potentially life-changing subject."

I nodded. My gut still was telling me it was a topic that would be life changing for her but not for me. I didn't need to enter the interior-design business for Kellie to see her dream fulfilled.

Then I remembered how I had used the same sort of reasoning when Kellie wanted to go in the hot-air balloon. I was immensely glad I had taken that risk. Would I feel the same way if I said yes to becoming her business partner? I definitely needed more time to think and pray about this.

The bus stopped near the impressive Marble Arch, and Kellie grabbed my arm. "Let's get off here."

"Here?"

She was already in the aisle. I stumbled down the steps in her wake and barely made it off the bus in the crush of people trying to get on.

"What's wrong?" I asked as soon as we were clear of the crowd.

"Shops!" she said brightly. "When I saw Marble Arch, I realized this is the start of Oxford Street. I read about it in your research material. This is the place for us to shop."

I did love the idea of coming home with something new to wear, especially a new pair of all-purpose jeans. Whenever I wore them, I would remember they came from London, and I would smile.

"Is this okay with you?"

"It's great, Lady Ebb. Lead the way."

We entered the first large department store we came to and found it had the same layout and feel of any major department store at home. Making our way to women's clothing, I slipped into my treasure hunt mode and headed for the clearance rack. My first find of the afternoon was a selection of raincoats half off the original price.

"Kellie, look." I held up the coat I liked so she could see the label. "It's a London Fog coat!"

"Perfect! You have to buy it."

I bought the coat along with a light cream-colored, button-up sweater. The sweater was more than half off and was made from a scrumptious blend of cashmere and merino wool. As soon as I tried it on, I felt warm. Warmer than I had felt since we had arrived. I determined to wear that sweater at all times during the rest of the trip unless the sun made another dazzling appearance. With this sweater and raincoat, I finally was ready for London.

Now the challenge was to find something I could wear fairly often once I got home. I told Kellie I wanted to have the chance to one day say, "Oh, this old outfit? Yes, this is the one I bought in London."

Such snootiness, she assured me, would only be acceptable with my closest family members and, of course, with her.

Kellie found a turtleneck and a scarf she liked. I copied her scarf inspiration and added a pair of socks that came with a label identifying their "perfect blend" of angora and cotton. Then I grabbed a plain white cotton T-shirt and headed to the cash register.

"What about jeans?" Kellie asked.

"I'm not in the mood. I think I can get by the next two days with these pants. I have a skirt with me too."

She gave me a skeptical look, and I knew what she was thinking. The way things had been going, it could be a challenge for me to keep my singular pair of pants out of harm's way.

"I know," I told her. "I should have packed another pair."

"That's not what I was going to say. I was going to say you really should take ten minutes, try on some jeans, and if you find any you like, great. If not, at least you tried."

That day, having a friend who was more persistent than I was proved useful. The second pair of jeans I tried on fit great, and I bought them. There, mission accomplished. I tucked my lightweight travel jacket into one of the shopping bags and tried out my London Fog raincoat. Just right.

Back out into the street we went. Both of us now had on raincoats with hoods, so we were ready to ward off the drops. The wet stuff was coming down in silver beads that looked as if they had been flung our way from around the neck of Madam Icicle of the Outer Hebrides.

We didn't get "pretty" raindrops like this in Florida. Where we lived, the sky wrung itself out in downpours during the wet season and duplicated a moist terrarium during several months on either side of the torrents.

Here, the rain seemed to have a different personality. It was purposeful but came with a playful twinkle. A Tinker Bell sort of rain.

Kellie's idea about hopping on and off the bus was a good one. When a bus for our desired route showed up again, we bustled our way on more aggressively than we had the first time. We tried again for seats up top and found we had to settle for holding on. At the next stop, though, two teens with spiked hair and earphones got off, and Kellie and I took their seats.

The bus rolled down Park Lane, a wide thoroughfare that leads directly to Buckingham Palace. We had a great view as we approached the imposing home of Britain's sovereigns for almost two hundred years. The Victoria Memorial, crafted of white marble at the base and topped with a golden-winged statue, was much larger and more imposing than the pictures I had seen. The memorial created a traffic roundabout and provided great pictures, as Kellie and I snapped away through the rain-dotted windows. I felt like a true tourist. And I didn't mind a bit.

At the front of the palace grounds, red-uniformed guards were posted at the closed black gate. Behind them loomed the decidedly rectangular, immensely large Buckingham Palace. Annette's term for Windsor Castle applied here as well. Buckingham Palace had a "strong beauty" to it. I was sure that the interior was even more impressive than the exterior, just as Windsor had been.

The bus kept going, and we made our way toward the river.

"Are we going to be able to see Big Ben from here?" Kellie pulled out the map. She quickly answered her own question. "No. We're heading south of Westminster and the Houses of Parliament. Wait. I have an idea. Let's get off at the next stop."

I followed my inspired friend, not sure what she was up to. The rain had stopped, and the clouds seemed to be clearing, but the light of day was waning.

"Should I ask what you're thinking?"

Kellie's eyes took on a mischievous twinkle. "No, I want to see if I can surprise you. Just follow me, and don't ask any questions."

"All right, bossy babe."

"You won't be badgering me a short time from now. That is, if my little scheme succeeds. If it doesn't work, then you can scoff at me all you want."

"That sounds like a fair deal," I said with a grin.

Kellie led us to the Victoria underground station. She bought the tickets for us, checked the map, and led the way down to where the next underground train to Westminster Station was boarding.

"Perfect timing," Kellie said. "Come on."

We slipped inside just as the doors closed, and we held on to a pole in the crowded compartment for the jostling ride. I switched my shopping bag to the other hand. I had combined all my purchases and was carrying them and my purse in one large, handled bag. The consolidation made it easier to be sure I had everything, but the weight seemed to have done a number on my wrist.

"You okay?" Kellie asked.

"I'm carrying too much in one bag," I said in a low voice. "I'll divide it up when we get out."

"Here, let me carry it. Just for a little while. That way I'll be balanced on both sides. You can give your hands a rest, and then in half an hour or so, we'll switch, and you can carry both bags for a while."

I liked her idea. "Ebb and Flo," I said and handed her my weighty bag. It felt odd suddenly to have my hands free.

We rode only as far as the next stop. Kellie motioned to me that we were getting off here. She secured a firm grasp on both our bags and made her way toward the open door. I was right behind her until a large woman with a fussing toddler in her arms pressed in front of me and then seemed to stop. I couldn't see around her to know if other passengers were bottlenecked in front of her or what was going on.

"Excuse me." I tried to maneuver around her so I could jockey my way to the door.

She didn't seem to hear me, nor did she move. I literally pressed my body sideways between the woman and a man who was wearing a heavy coat that smelled like wet wool and soaked mothballs. The damp odor rubbed off on my new raincoat. I felt desperate to reach the door. A swarm of business-clad passengers was pushing into the cabin. I could see Kellie already out on the platform looking around for me with a panicked expression.

"Kellie!" I pushed as forcefully as I could and reached the sliding doors as they came together and, like a cruel guillotine, severed me from Kellie. We were packed in, body to body, with no respectable breathing space. I pounded my fist on the closed door. It wouldn't budge.

The train moved forward, and I had no way to stop it.

Nineteen

Kellie and I made eye contact through the window. She shouted something, but I couldn't hear her. An instant later the train entered a tunnel, and everything outside our sardine can went dark.

Don't panic. Think. Think.

Kellie and I never had been in a situation like this, so I didn't have a precedent to refer to. We didn't have an arranged meeting place or a backtrack plan. I supposed the safest thing to do would be to get off at the next station, turn around, and go back to where Kellie was standing when the train pulled away. Without the familiar convenience of instant cell phone connection, I was lost.

I decided that if Kellie wasn't still standing where I last saw her, then I would take a cab back to our hotel. I would wait for her in our room. If she didn't return to the room right away, at least I could ask the concierge to help me.

My racing heart calmed as I repeated the logical plan to myself. Then I remembered. Kellie had my bag.

My purse was in the bag.

All I had with me were the clothes I was wearing.

I had been carrying a small stash of emergency money in the inside pocket of my jacket, but I had exchanged the jacket for the new raincoat. And all I had in the pocket of the raincoat was a wad of gray lint.

Oh boy, this isn't good. Lost in London. Not good. What do I do? What do I do?

The train slowed, and I knew my first step was to get out. I couldn't stand the claustrophobic conditions another minute. As soon as the door was halfway open, I slid out.

A recorded voice we had heard every time we boarded a train in the underground seemed to mock me as I stepped onto the cement platform: "Mind the gap." The bloodless voice was referring to the gap between the train and the platform. It wasn't a large space, but it certainly was wide enough for a wrong-turned foot to get wedged in.

I made sure to mind the gap as well as to mind my disoriented sense of direction. The first thing I did was stop in front of an underground map and determine which station I had just come from.

"Westminster," I said aloud. I saw that I had gotten off at Embankment. All I needed to do was wind my way up through the layered maze of stairs and escalators and board a train from the same Green Line going in the opposite direction.

My logic worked. I meandered my way through the concrete catacombs, found the platform for the next train back to Westminster, and waited for its arrival.

A rainstorm of possibilities pelted my thoughts. *What do I do if she isn't there? What if I can't find the right platform? What if she exited the underground?*

The strangest peace rested on me. As confusing and disconcerting as all this was, I felt as if every step I was taking was being protected. I didn't know exactly what I was doing. I didn't know where I was going. But I wasn't alone. More than I had ever experienced before, I was aware of the Lord's presence.

I boarded the train heading back to Westminster and thought, *When was the last time I felt this secure?*

I held on as the train took off, and the first part of the verse I had read in Exeter Chapel came back to me. *"I will give them a heart to know me, that I am the Lord."*

That's what was happening. I was recognizing that, even in this situation, Jesus Christ was Lord. And He was with me. I wasn't about to stand up and applaud like the man from Ireland had done in the theater, but inside, my heart was kneeling in humble adoration of the King of kings. I knew He wouldn't leave me.

Exiting at Westminster with renewed strength and more aggressive skills in place this time, I looked right and left for Kellie. I waited for the crowd to subside and walked to the end of the platform and back.

"Okay, what now, Lord?"

I went over to the map on the wall and looked for clues. *Why did Kellie want to get off here? What was it she wanted to keep as a surprise from me? What was her clever plan?*

Using my best Sherlock Holmes powers of deductions, I pulled together everything I knew about this part of London based on what I remembered from travel brochure photos and my Internet research.

Of course! Westminster. The Houses of Parliament. That means Ben is directly above me. Kellie was trying to arrange it so we would pop out of the underground station and be face to face with Ben.

Since no one was standing close enough to hear me, I raised my chin in satisfaction of a mystery well solved and said, "Elementary, my dear Watson."

Then I took off with purpose, certain that Kellie would know I had figured out her plan and would come looking for her under Ben's watchful gaze.

My optimistic steps took me as far as the exit of the Westminster underground. To leave the station, I needed to insert my ticket into the automatic turnstile that opens only after being fed the tiny slip of paper with the magnetic strip.

Thinking always of safety and potential pickpockets, I had placed my ticket securely inside the zippered pouch on the side of my purse. The very same purse that was now riding around with Kellie inside my heavy shopping bag.

I was stuck in the London underground. I couldn't get out!

"Excuse me." I stopped a woman who appeared to be close to my age. She was carrying a plastic grocery sack and a large box that had a picture of a toaster oven on the outside. She looked frazzled and in a hurry, but I imposed on her anyway. "I lost my ticket. Do you know how I can get out?"

"Find your ticket," she said brusquely and moved on through the turnstile without ever making eye contact with me.

I noticed a uniformed man in a bright green vest. "Excuse me, sir. I've lost my ticket. Can you tell me how I can get out?"

The walkie-talkie on his belt crackled, and he turned down the volume. "Did you have a ticket when you got on?"

"Yes. I left it in my bag."

"And where is your bag now?"

I should have considered my answer more carefully before saying to him in a lighthearted tone, "I don't know. It could be anywhere."

He removed the walkie-talkie from his belt and issued some sort of coded message before turning to me and saying, "Follow me, will you?"

I assumed he was taking me to the employee exit or some such exit for emergencies. Instead he ushered me into a small, enclosed office where two guards were standing next to a metal chair.

"Would you mind having a seat?" he asked. The other security personnel in the bright green vests both had their arms crossed and were giving me stern looks.

"What's going on?"

"Security measures. Please have a seat."

The door opened, and a uniformed bobby entered wearing black pants, a black hat, and a bright green, high-visibility jacket. He looked like the sort of officer who would be on international TV news reports explaining why a bomb squad had been called in to avert a potential disaster.

"Good evening," he said to me politely. "May we have a look at your ID?"

"I-I don't have it with me." For the past two days I had given up the pouch around my neck and had tucked my passport into my purse, just as the young woman had suggested when we were standing in line at customs.

"You're not carrying your passport?" he asked before I had a chance to explain.

"No, I had it with me, but it's in my bag."

"And your bag is…"

I decided I better talk fast. "I don't know. It's with my friend. She was carrying it for me, and I didn't make it off the train fast enough. She got off at Westminster, and I didn't. I went on to the next stop and then turned around and came back, but she wasn't there. I'm not sure I was even on the right platform. At this point

I don't know where she is. I thought she might be with Ben by now, but I couldn't get out to see."

"With Ben?" the officer asked.

"Big Ben." I realized these men were unlikely to understand my crush on a clock.

"Are you saying you were going to meet your friend at the Parliament Building?"

"I'm not sure she's there. I was just going to see if that's where she went."

"With your bag."

"Right. She was trying to surprise me, and I'm pretty sure the surprise was to see Big Ben."

"That was her surprise? To see Big Ben?"

I nodded and said in my fifteen-year-old voice, "I've never seen him before."

By that point even I was beginning to question my story. Big Ben is, well, big. He's hard to miss. Going to "see" him wasn't exactly a normal kind of surprise. These officials had reason to question me, but I wanted to make it clear that all they needed to do was let me out of the underground labyrinth, and I wouldn't bother them anymore. I was about to promise that I wouldn't even take the underground again during the rest of my time in London. I would stick to the buses and cabs and keep my passport on me at all times. But apparently it wasn't going to be that easy.

"Listen," the officer said. "I do believe your account of being separated from your friend. Quite common. But I'm afraid we're going to have to take our usual precautions and file a report."

"A report for what?"

"We're required to report all potential terrorist activity. This tube station has been on high alert the past few days, and we must report anything suspicious."

"Suspicious?" I stared at the man in disbelief. "Me?"

It took almost an hour for me to comply with all their questions and forms. The more my story unfolded, the more sympathy I seemed to gain from at least one of the officers. He said I was the most "winsome" tourist they had questioned in a long while.

I wasn't sure what that meant, but I was relieved when the bobby said he was going to call the hotel I listed to see if I was registered there. A few minutes later he returned to the small interrogation room confirming that, yes, my story matched up regarding the hotel. I understood now why the front desk had taken our passports at check-in and logged the information on them. I was registered officially with the hotel and that might have been the main reason they agreed to release me. That, and Kellie having left a message at the hotel in case I called in. The message was that she would meet me at the hotel.

Papers signed, case closed, I was released. One of the security officers used a master pass to activate one of the turnstiles, and I was set free. The minute I was on the other side, I turned back to him. "Oh, excuse me. I don't have any way of getting back to my hotel."

He looked down at my legs, as if to make sure I realized they were still attached and serviceable.

"Never mind," I said politely, realizing my issues were no longer his problem.

"I'll give you a pass just this once," he said as I was about to walk away. "Go back to Embankment, then take the Northern Line to Tottenham Court. You'll be all right from there."

The underground pass he handed me came with a friendly warning to keep this one in my pocket.

I thanked him and made my way into the belly of the earth beneath London. When I thought about it, having such an elaborate transportation system run extensively under the surface of this major city was pretty astounding.

The other astounding thing, I realized when I figured out how to make the change at Embankment, was that I was navigating these concrete-lined arteries of London. A few days ago I was hesitant to take a ride in a hot-air balloon. I had told Kellie I was afraid of defying gravity. That fear was gone. The Lord had been with me, guiding me, just as He had been every step of this trip. It had been many years since I had felt this close to Him.

The second half of the Jeremiah verse was becoming truer in my life than it ever had before: "They will be my people, and I will be their God, for they will return to me wholeheartedly."

What was happening inside me definitely was encompassing my whole heart.

With quiet confidence and nothing in the world but the clothes on my back and the underground pass in my pocket, I boarded the Northern Line train and took one of the open seats with the self-assurance of someone who did this every day.

When I disembarked at Holborn, I walked out to the street and looked around. It was dark now. I recognized the station since Kellie and I had started our daily adventures from this station twice. I started walking, and two blocks later I turned and walked another block and a half. There was our hotel—as grand as it had been when we first arrived in the taxi.

I went to the front desk to ask for a duplicate key. Before the clerk ran one of the credit card–sized keys through the machine for me, the hotel manager cordially stepped over and with a formal expression asked, "How are you this evening?"

"Fine," I said. And I meant it.

I took the elevator up to our floor and inserted the key in the door. Kellie must have heard the key because she rushed to the door and greeted me with a wild hug and expressions of relief. We talked over each other's sentences while still standing in the hall.

"How did you get back here? You didn't have your purse—"

"And I didn't have my tube ticket."

"I didn't realize I had your purse until I got back here to the room and dropped the bags on the floor, and there it was—"

"I tried to figure out where you wanted to take me—"

"I was saying to come back to the hotel. That's what I was yelling through the closed doors as the train pulled away: 'Go back to the hotel.'"

"I thought you were planning for us to come up from the underground station and see Big Ben."

"That was my original plan. How did you get out of the underground station without—"

"I asked for help and ended up being questioned as if I were a potential terrorist!"

"What!"

The door next to ours opened and shut soundly. It seemed our neighbors were giving us a subtle hint that we were being too noisy in the hallway. Covering our mouths, we took our debriefing session inside our room and closed the door.

We quickly agreed that staying in and ordering room service was a good option for us that evening. We had had enough excitement for one day.

Twenty

"Tell me again why we're getting up so early," I said the next morning after our wake-up call rang at five o'clock.

"The brochure says it's best to get an early start for the Portobello Road Antiques Market." Kellie had picked up a brochure in the hotel lobby the day before while waiting for me to arrive. The brochure promised us that all the fruit stalls and bakeries in Notting Hill offered their freshest wares first thing in the morning. "Some of the stalls open at 5:30 a.m. on weekends."

Kellie's determination paid off. When we arrived at 6:05, the place already was hopping. My impression of Portobello Road came from the movie *Notting Hill*. As it turned out, the images in the film mirrored the real-life experience quite closely. A few vendors still were unpacking their wares, but most of them were in full commerce swing when we strolled by the small, charming stalls.

We found a bakery on the corner that was doing a brisk business inside and had a cart set up outside laden with freshly baked goods. The croissants were as large as my outspread hand, and the ones filled with almond paste looked decadently delicious. We took two of those.

Then we found a tiny coffee bean store that had a long line of customers out the front door—neighborhood groupies waiting impatiently for their morning cup of joe. We soon knew what the attraction was. The fragrance of the dark ground coffee beans lingered in the nippy morning drizzle and surrounded that particular corner of the block like a promise of sunbeams in a cup.

We succumbed easily. Ten minutes later, with steamy, foamy lattes in one hand and big, fat, crumbly almond croissants in the other, we left the fruit and vegetable section of Portobello Road and journeyed into antique enlightenment as we strolled through the endless stalls. Anything, and I do mean anything, an antique seeker was looking for could be found somewhere within the jumbled, endearing maze of treasures.

When I pause now and remember all the delights of our trip to London, that morning, weaving through the indoor and outdoor booths with our coffee and croissants, oohing and aahing at every turn, well… I smile one of my best smiles every time I think about it.

The rain strolled right along with us all morning. I had on my new London Fog raincoat with the handy-dandy hood, so I didn't mind the drops or the drips. Underneath the wonderful coat I wore my new jeans and my new cashmere–merino wool sweater. I was happy. I was comfortable and full of contentment.

Kellie and I loved observing all the amazing people, particularly the vendors, who showed up here every day, rain or shine. They seemed to be barely affected by the swarms of people pressing their faces into the tiny stalls and picking up various items from the collections for inspection.

An odd china cup and saucer from a long-since-discontinued nineteenth-century Spode pattern was filled with antique earrings from the art deco era. The bejeweled items were tagged as coming from the estate sale of some lord and lady in the Lake District. Resting comfortably under the fine china cup was a dilapidated copy of John Bunyan's *Pilgrim's Progress,* complete with etchings, copyright 1845.

For the serious or even the casual collector of anything old, this was the one place in the world where that collector might find her elusive treasure.

Kellie and I bought a lot that day. We didn't spend an outrageous amount of money, but we bought a lot of treasures. Our treasure hunt started with a ring.

"Look at this," I said to Kellie when I spotted the darling ring in one of the indoor stalls. Sitting on a faded blue velvet pincushion, the ring looked like a dainty Miss Muffet sitting on her tuffet. The curds and whey were missing, but I'm sure a spider had sat down beside her more than once during her captivity in this haphazard display.

"Very dainty," Kellie commented. "Is that a tiny garnet?"

The vendor looked up. "That's a ruby chip. Handcrafted in the late eighteen hundreds and guaranteed eighteen-carat gold. Have a look."

He handed over a magnifying glass and pointed out the hammered marks and the tiny seal of the craftsman engraved inside the small ring.

"I picked it up at an estate sale in Rochester," he said. "Does give one pause to wonder, doesn't it? A ring like this made a century ago could have been an engagement ring for a country girl."

I was smitten. The sweet little ring had to come home on my finger so I could gaze at it on dreary days and wonder about the woman who wore it first and what she thought about on dreary days.

"How much do you want for it?" I asked the dealer. He could have said a hundred pounds, and at that point in my sweet infatuation, I would have considered the price a bargain. It turned out the cost was the equivalent of twenty dollars.

The amiable vendor polished the ring with a stained white handkerchief, took my cash, and placed the trinket in the palm of my hand. No box. No wrapping. No receipt. This was flea-market shopping in its most primitive and intoxicating form.

We walked away, with me admiring my new little accessory and Kellie saying, "I can't believe the price was so low."

"I know. You do realize that for a hunt-and-gather girl like me, this place is the mother lode."

"I think this is treasure hunting at its sweetest and best."

Of course I agreed. With my ring at home on my pinkie finger, I felt as if every ten-pound note in my pocket needed to be exchanged as ransom for other such prize beauties.

Kellie was the one who scored next. Her find was an antique Moroccan mirror in a frame inlaid with bits of pounded silver and glass. The mirror was the size of a greeting card, and for such compactness, the intricate details were captivating.

We meandered from store to store and stall to stall for hours, snagging books, beaded bracelets, candlesticks, and decorated tin boxes that once held buttery biscuits most likely served at teatime.

The crowds around us swelled. The weight of our shoulder bags grew heavy. We felt hot under our raincoats every time we entered one of the strings of indoor booths, and we were crushed by people every time we stepped back into the main thoroughfare. But we couldn't stop. Hunting and gathering was my thing. Feasting on color, shape, and design was Kellie's thing. We were in our elements at the same time.

My watch said it was 1:06 p.m. when Kellie and I finally hit our limit.

"We have to leave something for us to come back and find another time," Kellie said.

"Another time? Are you already thinking about coming back to London?"

She nodded with an I'm-so-in-love-with-this-place smile on her face.

"Me too." I didn't open up the conversation then in the crowded marketplace, but I was also thinking about something else. I was thinking about Kellie's proposal to go into business together. After the way we had been so in step with each other throughout the market that morning, it made me wonder if we really could run a business together.

We stopped at an organic café next to the Scottish kilt shop and ordered fresh-squeezed orange juice and garden salads to revive us. Our debate du jour was whether we should make a beeline to see Ben from here or return to the hotel and drop off our bags.

The return-to-the-hotel option won. As much as we wanted to cram every minute of our final day in London with all we could see and do, we had turned ourselves into pack mules, and neither of us wanted to lug our loot across London.

"Aside from Ben, what's left on our list?" Kellie asked after we had stashed our treasures and stretched out on our beds for a two-minute refresher.

"Westminster Abbey, which is conveniently located right next to Ben. Do you realize we've managed to do everything on our top-five lists?"

"I know. I can't believe how much we've seen and done in such a short time," Kellie said. "You ready to foray back into the London maze?"

"Ready and eager."

But as we walked through the hotel lobby, Kellie and I were

delayed. Afternoon tea had commenced in the conservatory, and as we walked by, we knew the dainties that awaited us on the other side of that open door.

"What do you think?" Kellie asked as we stood there. "It's your choice. This might be our last chance to have a proper teatime in London."

"I'm not that hungry after our salad, but it's like you said, this is our last chance to have tea in London. At least a fancy teatime."

I peeked inside the conservatory room where harp music filled the room, as did an assortment of men and women and a few children sitting at the round, linen-covered tables with admirable posture and quiet voices.

"No," I said. "We've experienced that adventure already. Let's go see Ben."

"So it's boys over food," Kellie said. "Now you're acting like the fifteen-year-old who never gave up her first crush."

I shrugged playfully, and off we went, fearlessly taking the underground to Westminster and going through the motions as if we knew exactly what we were doing. In a poetic-justice sort of way, I suppose we did know what we were doing. This was familiar territory now. We both had been this way before. Just not together.

I watched the faces of the people on the underground. Such an amazing variety.

Kellie and I exited without causing any sort of potential international incident, which was refreshing, and took the steps up to the sidewalk. Like hibernating cave dwellers, we came out into the daylight and blinked in the brightness.

And there he was.

Looming straight, tall, and proud, with the late afternoon sky behind him turning a gentle shade of forget-me-not blue, Ben didn't flinch.

I smiled.

"He's handsome," Kellie said.

"Yes, he is."

We stood on a busy street corner, staring at the golden boy while double-decker red buses went through their daily paces and round-nosed black taxicabs carried important people to important meetings in important buildings.

"Do you want to get up close and personal with him first, or should we try to get into Westminster Abbey?"

I was torn. He was right there. I could walk a few blocks and be at his feet. That moment would be the fulfillment of my forty-year wish. But I dearly wanted to see the Poet's Corner at Westminster Abbey. And if I remembered correctly, the Poet's Corner closed earlier than the rest of the Abbey.

"I think we'd better visit Westminster Abbey first," I said with a sigh. "I don't want to miss seeing the Poet's Corner."

"Ben will still be here when we come back."

We were about to cross the street and make our way to Westminster Abbey when Kellie said, "Wait. I see a photo op here." She scurried over to a red phone booth.

I was thinking we should get to the Poet's Corner first and take the phone booth picture later. The red booths were on nearly every street, so it wouldn't be hard to have a photo op just about anywhere around London.

"Stand right there." Kellie pulled out her camera.

"Wouldn't it better if I posed inside the booth?"

"No. Right there, outside the booth. Ready? Smile." She clicked the photo, had a look at it on her digital playback screen, and said, "Perfect. Now would you take one of me?"

We switched places, and the minute I lined up the camera to take the shot, I saw what Kellie had in mind. From this phone booth, the view of the side of Big Ben was ideal. Double-decker buses and London cabs flowed with the traffic in the street between us and the Houses of Parliament. Kellie had a good eye. I had always known that. She had picked a great location for a memorable shot of all that typifies London.

Picking up the pace, we arrived at the entrance to Westminster Abbey a slim three minutes before the final admittance into Poet's Corner. We entered the massive, ornate cathedral, and in a hushed voice, Kellie said, "Tell me what we're looking for in here. I didn't read anything about this place, so tell me what you know."

"I know that Westminster Abbey has been the location of Christian worship for more than a thousand years."

"Seriously?"

"It wasn't always this grand, of course."

"A thousand years. I can't even imagine that," Kellie said.

"I know. And if I remember correctly, this is where the sovereign rulers of Great Britain have celebrated coronations, burials, and all official ceremonies for hundreds of years."

"Were Charles and Diana married here?"

"No, that wedding was at St. Paul's Cathedral."

Glancing around inside the main area, we could see why St. Paul's was selected for Charles and Diana's wedding. Westminster Abbey was regal and reverence inducing with the rows of wooden pews and an impressive altar at the front. But it looked as if the seating could accommodate a thousand people at most. That may have been sufficient seating in ages past, but modern events of historic significance required space for multiple thousands.

I directed Kellie to hurry to the entry for the Poet's Corner. "This is where Chaucer was buried," I said. "After that, it became the favored location inside the abbey to bury other authors and poets."

"Remind me again who Chaucer was," Kellie whispered.

"The author of *The Canterbury Tales.*"

"Oh, right. So who else is buried here?"

"I don't remember, but I know that some authors are buried elsewhere, like Shakespeare, but they have a memorial here."

Kellie stopped walking on the echoing marble floors and looked around at the limestone walls and various statues. A soothing, golden glow came through a nearby window. The clouds had skipped out of town, and the sun was back, warming up the sky once again.

"This place has a strong beauty," she said. "Isn't that what Annette called it? This place feels old, solid, and strong."

We stepped over to a statue of Shakespeare and examined it.

"I wonder if he really looked like that," Kellie said. "Because I pictured him differently."

"In what way?"

"I think I've always pictured Shakespeare as the embodiment of all the strong characters he wrote about."

"If that were the case, in what ways do you think he would look different from this statue?" I asked.

"He would be a lot taller."

I smiled. "Hooray for modern medicine and vitamins."

"True."

We slowly made our way through the rest of the abbey, with Kellie going one direction while I went another. I was on my own literary appreciation tour. I looked down and saw a plaque inset in the floor. The name on the plaque was Charles Dickens. I smiled and whispered, "Thank you, my friend, for all the wonderful stories you wrote."

As I continued around the small chapel, I nodded at the Brontë sisters' memorial in the stained glass and said "thank you" to Rudyard Kipling for *The Jungle Book*. I winked at Jane Austen's memorial, feeling only pride and no prejudice against any of the collected authors in this small, sacred space.

These were the storytellers who had filled with hope the most challenging time of my life. I felt as if I had "met" all these dear people during my months of convalescence, and now I was here, alive and healthy four decades later. Their stories took me outside and away from my precarious illness. Today I was inside and near to the memory of what they had contributed to the world.

I stood back and took in the whole of the Poet's Corner. In my research the week before, I had concluded that the British Empire built its greatest monuments out of paper and pen since literature was England's longest-lasting contribution to history and the arts. Great Britain's literature had certainly made a long-lasting contribution to my life.

With a final smile of appreciation to the writers represented in this hallowed place, I thought, *Dearest England, you have a treasure box for your memories. And this is it.*

Kellie slid up next to me. "I'm ready to go when you are." Then she spotted the tears that had welled up in my eyes. "Are you okay?"

I nodded. Even my closest friend couldn't understand the happiness I felt in this place. That was okay. She didn't need to understand or even try to share it with me. This was a full circle for me, and I felt as if, in a sweet way, the Lord had given me this moment to remind me of His faithfulness over all these years. My dormant wish had come true at a time when I needed to believe all over again.

And what I found myself believing was that God, my heavenly Father and Lord, had His hand on my life. He had a few wishes yet to come true for me.

Twenty-One

With a smile still on my lips, I exited Westminster Abbey with Kellie close behind and stepped into the dusk of the calm London evening. The air had cooled, and waves of a faint scent of diesel rose from the damp asphalt. We were back in the real world.

"I have an idea," Kellie said. "This is along the lines of what I was trying to set up yesterday, but this time I won't keep it a surprise. I was thinking, what if we took the tube under the river, did a loop through Shakespeare's Globe Theatre, walked under the London Eye, and then came across the Westminster Bridge and got a view of Parliament and Big Ben from the riverside? Or we could take a bus over to St. Paul's, see if there's enough time to tour it, and then take a boat ride down the Thames and come toward Ben with a true river view. It could be dramatic."

I laughed. At the moment I thought Kellie was the one being dramatic, but I didn't mention that to her.

"What? I'm serious. I want this next encounter of yours with Big Ben to be memorable."

"It sounds like you've been spending way too much time with your map of London."

"That's what I was doing yesterday while I was in the hotel room praying you would find your way back. I was trying to figure out where you would get off, what you would do, and where I should look for you. That's when I realized how much more we need to see."

"I know, but, Kellie, really, it's enough. Everything we've seen and done so far. It's enough. It's bountiful. All I want to do now is take a closer look at Ben and take a bunch of pictures. I'll go home tomorrow a content woman. Besides, what was it you said earlier about needing to leave a few things for when we come next time?"

"You're right. One day I would love to come back."

"Me too."

Kellie's shoulders relaxed. "I'm glad you said that, Liz. My senses are beginning to hit overload."

The closer we walked to the River Thames, the more we commented on how the Houses of Parliament stretch much farther along the waterfront than we had imagined from the photos. They reminded me of an enormous sandcastle, complete with turrets, towers, and that great golden shade of summer wheat. And there, at the forefront of this masterpiece, stood Ben with his ornate spire piercing the evening sky.

We made our way to the other side of the very busy intersection by taking an underground walkway that brought us up at the beginning of the Westminster Bridge, directly across the street from the monolith.

I stepped closer to the bridge's edge, away from the dense stream of pedestrians. Planting my feet, I pulled out my camera, ready for my first shot.

But then, realizing we hadn't been properly introduced yet, I gazed up one more time at Mr. Tall, Dark, and Handsome, and with the timidity of a fifteen-year-old, I said, "Hello."

At that moment something magical happened.

Ben's face lit up.

"Did you see that?" Kellie had just snapped a picture of me in front of Ben.

I laughed. "It's just like my poem!"

"What poem?"

"I didn't tell you? Mrs. Roberts had me write a poem about Big Ben. I'm not sure I remember all of it."

"Well, try," Kellie said, caught up in the charm of the moment.

"It was something like,

'Your strong, straight arms will welcome me
when at last we meet.
I'll hear your deep, resounding voice
from way across the street.
And when I see your handsome face

light up just for me,
I'll know that this is not just a crush
because I will feel such glee.'"

Kellie laughed uproariously.

"I was fifteen," I protested, feeling my cheeks burn.

"No, I'm not laughing at you. I love it! His face did light up just for you."

I looked up at him again. "Yeah, it did, didn't it?"

We were like two schoolgirls on the playground. I had a crush on Ben, and he had acknowledged my adoration by lighting up and smiling back at me. It was all very silly, I know, but that face-to-face encounter was above and beyond anything I had ever hoped.

Kellie and I snapped pictures like crazy, caught up in the delight of the moment. We bent backward for long shots, we knelt down for upward shots. We did zooms and tried out the special sepia-tone feature on Kellie's camera.

The sky seemed to be in on the stage direction because it provided the perfect evening backdrop. The violet shades had deepened and were now streaked with fluttering ribbons of elongated pink and orange clouds. As the daylight dimmed, a few stars appeared. We didn't know if they would show up in the pictures, but we tried to capture them in the shots.

"Isn't there a line in *Peter Pan* about 'take the first star and turn right'?" Kellie asked.

"The line is, 'second star to the right and straight on 'til morning.' That's what Peter Pan says when he flies past Big Ben with Wendy and the boys on their way to Neverland. And look at you, quoting British literature. Kellie, I'm impressed!"

"*Attempting* to quote British literature. It's your influence on me this week."

We silently gazed at the scene before us that was much grander than anything I had pictured in my imagination when Peter Pan sprinkled pixie dust on the Darling children and they flew with him all the way to Neverland. This night, in the real world, with the breathtaking sky spread so generously over London's rooftops, I thought how the stars looked like glittering jewels in an unseen crown that drifted in the heavens just over the top of Big Ben.

"Do you want to hear what I've been thinking?" Kellie asked.

"Always."

"I was thinking of the guy who sat by you at *Les Misérables* and how we were trying to remember that verse about every knee bowing to Jesus Christ and declaring Him as Lord."

"I've thought about that since the play as well."

"Well, I'm just thinking how incredible that day is going to be when we do finally see Christ face to face. I mean, here we are, all choked up over the face of a clock and what this moment represents to you. But think of what it's going to be like when we stand before Almighty God, the Ruler of all powers and principalities, and look into His face at last."

Neither of us spoke for a long moment.

"Hmmm," Kellie murmured.

I noticed she had a funny little grin on her face.

"What?"

"I don't mean to sound silly at a moment like this, but Peter Pan only got to fly away to Neverland. When we go to be with the Lord, we get to fly away to Everland!"

I smiled back at my witty friend. It had been years since I had felt this sense of delight when it came to talking about God. Everything about my faith felt new again and fresher than ever.

The rosy glow lingered the rest of our final night in London. We strolled for hours over the Westminster Bridge and then back up the road to Trafalgar Square, where we took flash-assisted photos under the great lion statues and dipped our fingers in the fountain under the gaze of the immensely tall statue of Lord Nelson.

We returned to the hotel and reluctantly packed our suitcases before we went to bed so we could start our trek back to Olney early in the morning.

Our familiarity with the various modes of transportation helped as we took the underground, then a train, then a coach, and then a cab that pulled up at Rose's front door.

I smiled when my feet touched the "Go Away" mat. Such wit. Did I understand it entirely after such a short visit? No. But I felt at home in the humor and in the breakfast room of Rose's cottage.

Rose greeted us affectionately, which was a bit of a surprise.

She had prepared a pot of tea, of course, and had everything ready for us when we arrived. Opal remained in the bedroom, scurrying to "collect her things." Kellie and I sipped a cheering cuppa with Rose while we waited.

"Virgil is determined to drive you to the airport," Rose said calmly. "I hope you don't mind."

"No, that's fine." Leaning closer I asked, "How did everything go this week between Virgil and Opal?"

Her eyes lit up. They looked just like Opal's shiny blue marble eyes looked when Virgil had entered the house before the pancake race with his floppy chef's hat on. "Why do you ask?"

"I had the impression Opal was sweet on Virgil and vice versa."

She blinked and appeared to blush. I couldn't believe how similar the twins' mannerisms were. They were probably even more in tandem after spending this time together.

Before Rose could give me the inside scoop, Opal shuffled into the breakfast room, and the first thing our eyes went to were her hot pink running shoes.

"Do you plan to run another race this morning?" Kellie asked.

I wanted to giggle, but I didn't.

"Only the race of life," Opal said philosophically. "My sister said they would be a good choice for the airport."

"I think Rose is right," I said.

"I hope she is this time." Opal gave a long, pensive sigh.

"I am." Rose smiled with confidence. She got up from her chair easily while her sister scowled.

What had the two sisters disagreed over now? Kellie and I had speculated earlier that it might be difficult for the two of them to part ways, but it seemed they were ready to return to their lives on either side of the Atlantic.

"Virgil should be here any moment." Rose began to clear the table.

Kellie and I offered to help Opal with her luggage. By the time we had wrestled her bag to the car, Virgil was standing by the boot, finding creative ways to make all of it fit. He greeted us cheerfully as usual. "Your carriage awaits, your majesty."

Opal looked at Virgil with a shadow of disapproval. In that one look was the answer to my question: love had not blossomed between these two. Hope, it seemed, did not spring eternal.

I returned to the front door, where Rose looked on, her expression reflecting a soft glow. She seemed much more agreeable than she had when we first arrived. I gave her a hug and thanked her again for her gracious hospitality.

Reaching for my hand, she said, "Elizabeth, my dear, do you know what the dearest kindness is that a woman can offer herself in the autumn of her years?"

I shook my head. It seemed odd that she was calling me Elizabeth, the way Virgil did.

"It is the gift of giving herself permission to take risks."

And then she winked at me.

Kellie was behind me. She gave Rose her thanks, accompanied by a warm hug. "We'll take care of your sister."

Rose grinned. "She's quite capable of taking care of herself. I'm sure she'll make that clear soon enough."

We squished into the backseat with our smaller pieces of luggage, and with a final wave, we were off to the airport, this time without Boswald.

As we drove past the impressive parish church that had been the location of the pancake breakfast after the race, Kellie said, "I'm surprised that your church is so large. We visited several churches in Oxford, and all of them were more the size of chapels."

"We had a famous minister," Opal said. "Have you heard of John Newton?"

I thought I had, but I didn't know why his name sounded familiar. Kellie answered no for both of us.

"Perhaps you know some of his hymns."

Without further prompting, Virgil broke into a deep-voiced rendition of "Amazing Grace" while Opal shot him disagreeable glances.

"I've always loved that hymn," Kellie said.

"He wrote that about the time you Yanks were busy trying to make a break from King George and form your own independent nation," Opal added as commentary. "Newton was a slave trader, you know. Not quite the reputable hymn writer one might expect."

"Yes," Virgil added. "Yet from such a background comes appreciation for grace, don't you think?" He caught my eye in the rearview mirror.

I nodded, and as if that was the only invitation he needed, Virgil said, "The twins knew me in my former days. Hooligan that I was, you might say I've come to acquire an appreciation for grace, just as Newton did."

Opal was staring out the window, purposefully not engaged in Virgil's tiny confession, even though it was the sanest collection of sentences we had heard him offer during our short acquaintance.

With a glance at Opal, he added wistfully, "A great strength lies in letting go of what was past and entering what is now. We all are given only so many days on this earth."

Opal seemed unaffected by his words. If that was his last-ditch effort to garner her affection, the attempt had failed. Poor Virgil. There was so much to love about this strong, individualistic man.

Neither Kellie nor I tried to enter the conversation that seemed to be taking place between the lines and in the front seat only. But we exchanged looks, as if both of us were keenly aware of the way Rose's slightly sour attitude had rubbed off on her twin during their time together.

Virgil didn't say another word until he offered his farewell to us at the airport. The good-bye to Opal was stiff and involved no eye contact. The eternal romantic in me felt a soft sadness. I had hoped the two of them would share a sweet sort of renewed love during their time together. Apparently Cupid's arrows had missed their mark.

Twenty-Two

A week after we returned home and had our lives back to something that resembled normalcy, Kellie and I met at our usual time at Brew-La-La. The cranberry red chairs were vacant, waiting for us. Nothing else about our lives felt the same.

We stood staring at the familiar menu board, trying to decide what to order. The barista recognized us and asked, "Should I start the usual for you both?"

"No," I said. "I'm not sure what I want, but I know I want to try something different."

"Do you have any tea?" Kellie asked.

The barista looked offended.

"I'll just have—"

"A Valencia mocha." I selected the first item on the house specialty list.

"Make that two of those," Kellie said.

For years I had skimmed the six specialty drinks, wondering what they tasted like, but I never had been willing to risk trying one in case I didn't care for it. But that was before I stepped into a hot-air balloon and went soaring over the Cotswolds.

"Did I ever tell you what Rose said to me the day we left?" I asked as Kellie and I settled into our conversation corner.

"I don't think so."

"She said the nicest gift a woman can give herself is to take risks. Something like that. She said it more eloquently."

"So that's why you're taking risks with the Valencia mocha?"

I told Kellie I now planned to work my way down the list.

"Well, I'll tell you how I'm planning to take a risk," Kellie said with a victorious grin. "I filed for a business license yesterday. K & L Interiors has moved out of the dream stage and is about to become reality."

I swallowed and leaned back in the chair. "K & L Interiors," I repeated. We hadn't had a final conversation about my involvement yet. I still was debating whether this was a risk I wanted to take.

"Kellie, I have to tell you something. I've thought about this a lot, and I don't want anything—especially business or money—to ever come into our friendship and separate us the way…"

"The way we got off track for those two years?"

I nodded. "I hated being in that awkward place. Absolutely hated it."

"That was a long time ago. We're not there now. We haven't been for decades."

Our coffees were ready. Kellie went to retrieve them, and I thought of how a small misunderstanding had placed the wedge between us. My husband and Kellie's husband had bumped heads over a business investment when both of us had been married only a few years. We lost a small amount of money in the deal, but at the time it represented a lot to us. Martin and Roger didn't want to socialize during the upheaval, so Kellie and I felt we couldn't pursue our budding friendship since our husbands weren't "bonding" as well.

Life went on. Kellie and I had babies, our paths as two families crossed frequently, and one day everything changed. The misunderstanding burned up in a heap of charcoal during a church picnic while Martin and Roger spent an hour flipping hamburgers next to each other, making amends over a flaming grill. From that day on we were friends again. All of us. Even our five children.

I learned then that men do friendship differently than women do. I also discovered that neither Roger nor Martin would have tried to deter us if Kellie and I had chosen to spend more time together. I gained many insights in the spring years, including that friendships can be fragile.

Now that we were entering our autumn years and Rose was telling me to take risks, I still didn't feel at peace about going into business with Kellie.

Kellie returned with the Valencia mochas. I thought I saw one of those I've-got-a-secret looks in her eyes. As she sat down across from me, she asked, "Do you feel as if we've thoroughly resolved our friendship disconnection from the past? I mean, the misunderstanding between Martin and Roger and the way that spilled over onto you and me?"

"Yes, definitely. I don't think we have anything to hash out, and I'm not saying I'm harboring any unresolved feelings. I'm just trying to say that I have strong hesitations about taking the risk of partnering in this new business because—"

"It's not your dream," she said softly.

I nodded. "It's your dream."

Kellie's eyes warmed. "And do you know what your dream is?"

I shook my head. I had been content to experience all the delights of my wish come true for the past few weeks. I didn't think I had a dream. "Do you think a dream is different than a wish?"

"I do," Kellie said. "I could be all wrong, but I think a wish is something whimsical you hope for when you blow out birthday candles or blow a dandelion in the breeze."

"As opposed to feeling a breeze and then sitting in a field of dandelions," I added with a wry grin.

She laughed. "Exactly. It seems that when a wish comes true, it's sweet and satisfying. And when it's over, that's it. But a dream is something that starts in the part of your heart where your passions lie. It doesn't go away."

"Do you think I have a dream and don't know it?"

Kellie's eyes did all the answering in the affirmative, but her lips stayed pressed to the edge of her to-go cup.

"What? What do you see that I don't?"

"First star on the right and the second cloud in the morning."

I shook my head. "No, it's 'second star to the right and straight on 'til morning.'"

"Exactly. Don't you see it? Liz, you have a passion for British literature. You need to do something with that."

"Like what?"

"I don't know. Read to children at the library. Teach a class at the community college on literature appreciation. Lead literary tours to London and visit all the homes of your favorite authors. Start a blog about Mary Poppins or something. I don't know. It's your dream. Go ahead and dream!"

I sat back, stunned and at the same time filled with a rising sense of adventure. "You're right. This is my passion, my dream. I've never done anything with it."

Kellie smiled and took a small sip of her coffee. "This is pretty good. The orange flavor is a little strong, but it's nice."

I wasn't interested in the coffee. I was interested in the topic. "Why didn't I ever see this before?"

"Maybe you had to go to England before you could see it. I certainly never saw it before in you. Then the minute we hit British soil, this wealth of information came popping out of you."

"So, wait. If this is my dream and I should figure out how to pursue doing something with this passion, what about you and the business? You said you got the license already. For K & L Interiors."

Kellie nodded. "L is for LeeAnne."

"Your daughter-in-law?"

It all made sense. The combination was brilliant, actually. LeeAnne and Kellie got along great. They lived four miles from each other. LeeAnne had majored in marketing and had spent the past three years working for a company that remodeled vacation rental homes.

"Kellie…"

"I know. It's perfect, isn't it?"

"You can still count on me to do some hunting and gathering, you know."

"I was hoping you would say that." Kellie looked down at her cell phone that was vibrating in the corner pocket of her purse. She read the incoming phone number. "It's Opal."

"Ask her if we can stop by this morning. I bought some gingersnaps yesterday and was thinking of checking on her."

"I was thinking the same thing." Kellie answered her phone. A moment later her eyebrows were pressing inward with concern.

"Everything okay?"

Kellie closed her phone. "Opal sounded frustrated. She hasn't been able to make her television work, and the staff at the manor has been no help in getting it fixed. I told her we would come over."

I was prepared to call the cable company once we arrived at Opal's apartment. The problem, however, was resolved once we showed her which buttons on her remote she needed to push to realign her television on the right cable channel.

"I brought you some biscuits." I pulled out the bag of gingersnaps.

"That was kind of you. Thank you."

We stood awkwardly waiting for what to do next. Opal didn't invite us to tea as she had in the past. Although, we always had arrived later in the afternoon, so perhaps it was too early for one of our little tea parties. I also noticed Opal seemed sad, less twinkle eyed than in the past.

"Is there anything else we can do for you while we're here?" Kellie asked.

"No, you were most kind to come right away."

"We were over at Brew-La-La," I said.

Opal didn't respond.

"The coffee café," I said.

Still no response.

"Where we met," Kellie added.

"Yes, of course." Her expression lightened a bit.

"We'll be on our way," Kellie said. "But call me anytime you want."

"We would be happy to come by for tea sometime," I said.

Opal nodded and saw us to the door.

Kellie and I made our way to the parking lot, and I said, "I hope she's okay. She doesn't seem herself."

"It could be the jet lag. It took me a few days to get back on track with sleeping and eating."

"The time with her sister really seemed to change her," I said. "Did you notice on the plane home she ordered chicken? On the flight to England she said she didn't care for the 'foul fowl.'"

"That's right. And she wanted the aisle seat on the way home too, which was different."

"I know. It's almost as if we brought the wrong twin home."

Kellie and I stopped in the middle of the parking lot and faced each other with stunned expressions. At the same moment we said, "We did! We brought home the wrong twin!"

Hustling back through the front doors of Sunshine Manor, we impatiently pressed the elevator button as if it would take us to Opal's floor sooner.

"Why would those two pixies do something like this?" Kellie asked.

"Virgil," I said with an air of assurance. "I bet Opal wanted to stay because of Virgil. Rose, for some reason, agreed to switch with her sister, but she's obviously not happy about it."

"Maybe they only had one passport between them. If Rose has never been outside of England, it could be that she had to travel on Opal's passport."

"Why, those…"

"What was it you told me that Rose, or maybe it was Opal, said to you at the front door when we were leaving the cottage?"

I snapped my fingers. "You're right! She said a woman should give herself permission to take risks. Then she winked at me. That's because she was taking a huge risk right before our eyes."

We arrived at the apartment front door, and Kellie whispered, "How can we be sure this is Rose?"

"We'll ask her."

"And hope she tells the truth."

The door opened. The twin—Rose, we presumed—looked at us with surprise and a twinge of irritation.

"We wanted to ask you something," Kellie said.

Remembering our debriefing session in the hallway of the fancy hotel in London after I returned from my escapade, I asked, "Would it be okay if we came in?" I didn't want the neighbors to hear our conversation.

The twin closed the door behind us. I suddenly thought to check her hand.

Opal wears the opal ring.

I saw only a thin gold band. No opal ring. The jig was up, whatever that meant. Sherlock Holmes himself would have been pleased with my powers of deduction.

Fortified with the evidence before me, I said, "Rose, why did you and Opal switch places?"

Kellie seemed stunned at my aggressive approach. Rose was stunned as well. She had to sit down. At first she wore a defiant look, as if she could bully her way out of the accusation. Then, just as instantly, the fight drained from her, and her confession tumbled forth as if it were Shrove Tuesday and the church bells had just rung.

"It wasn't my idea. It was Opal's. It seems my sister was determined to be with Virgil once she saw him again." Shaking her white, fluffed-up hair, she looked at us sorrowfully. "And you might as well know the worst of it."

"The worst of it?" Kellie repeated, eyebrows raised.

Rose sighed with forlorn exaggeration. "Opal means to marry the hooligan."

"She does?"

"Virgil? Opal and Virgil are getting married?" I said.

Rose responded with a single solemn nod.

"That's wonderful." Kellie turned to me. "Don't you think so?"

I smiled. "I think it's very sweet."

Rose took on a stern expression. "You wouldn't think so if you knew the sort of tomfoolery Virgil got into in his younger days. My sister had a secret affection for him even back then. But Father always said Virgil wouldn't amount to much. And he hasn't."

"Oh but, Rose, don't you see?" I asked. "Opal still cares about him. And Virgil cares about her. Why not bless this small wish of theirs to be together? Haven't you ever had a small wish you always hoped might somehow come true?"

She lowered her chin. "Yes."

"What was your wish?"

"It was my small wish that prompted me to agree to this exchange. I didn't have a passport, but I always wanted to see Disney World. That was my small wish."

Rose won my immediate empathy. I knew all about wishes. Especially ones that have hibernated for decades.

Rose straightened her shoulders. "All that aside, I know what my sister and I did was irresponsible and foolhardy. We intended to make things right soon enough. But that was before Opal phoned yesterday to say she's making wedding plans." Rose blinked. "I'm not quite sure what's to be done next."

Kellie and I sat for a moment, allowing the puzzle pieces to fall into their connecting places. The coziness of this mystery switched to lip-biting level as I realized we had assisted an illegal alien to enter the U.S. I had been questioned in London as a terrorist suspect. What would the government officials in my homeland have to say about this situation?

Before I could convey my concerns to Kellie, she turned to Rose and in Kellie's professional manner she said, "I'll tell you what's to be done next. You need to go put on your hot pink trainers."

Rose looked confused as well as disgruntled. "They are Opal's shoes, as you now know. And they are too small for me. I rubbed some terrible blisters on my feet on the way here."

Kellie laughed. "Then just go put on your most comfortable shoes, Rose. And grab your hat. Liz and I are taking you to Disney World. Right now."

"Now? But—" Rose pressed her hand against her flushed cheek.

"We'll rent a wheelchair," Kellie said.

I whispered to Kellie, "We have a few legal issues here. Don't you think we should—"

"Not yet. We'll address all that soon enough. First things first. This Sisterchick of ours has a wish that needs fulfilling, and for better or worse, I would say you and I are her fairy godmothers."

Epilogue

Five weeks after Kellie and I pushed Rose in a wheelchair around Disney World, we were back on a plane bound for Heathrow. This time our husbands were with us, and Rose was wearing her own appropriately sized hot pink tennis shoes. Our entourage was headed for a wedding at the Olney parish church.

Martin and Roger had worked together to help straighten out the awkward predicament Kellie and I inadvertently had caused when we brought the wrong twin back to Florida. Arrangements were made for the four of us to escort the petite culprit back to her rosy cottage, where she agreed to spend the remainder of her days living under her true identity. Opal and Virgil were content to live in Virgil's cottage, two hundred yards away from Rose's home and through a garden gate.

After Rose's joyful tour of Disney World, she had taken on a sweeter view toward her sister's dream of spending her winter years with Virgil. Rose was willing to add her blessing to the union.

Her sweetness remained and was put to good use when we arrived in Olney at her cottage. Opal was waiting for her, standing on the "Go Away" mat with her arms outstretched. Rose trotted up the path, and the two sisters greeted each other the way they probably should have six weeks earlier when we first arrived with Opal.

The wedding was like a scene out of a Jane Austen novel. Virgil waited at the front of the spacious church, exuding complete sense and sensibility in his respectable brown suit and focusing his affectionate smile on his demure bride. The little Florida orange blossom sashayed down the long center aisle toward her Mr. Darcy, the reformed yak, in a floor-length ivory skirt and a simple ivory sweater adorned with an antique collar of Olney lace that had belonged to her grandmother. On her feet, spunky Opal wore her hot pink tennies that peeked out with each step like timid twins looking for mischief.

"Look how she's holding the bouquet," Kellie whispered with a giggle. "It's the same way she held the frying pan in the pancake race. At least we can have no doubt that the right twin is marrying Virgil."

My favorite part of the service was when the guests were invited to stand and join in singing "Amazing Grace." I watched my dear husband choke up when he realized we were singing his favorite hymn inside the church where the song's composer had preached for nearly forty years.

The reception was held in a charming local teahouse called

Tea Cups. I watched as Virgil invited Rose to stand beside Opal in the receiving line. The two sisters beamed in their regal way, greeting their public, finishing each other's sentences, and glowing with equality.

Kellie commented on the transformation of the twins that evening as she, Martin, Roger, and I were on our way to our London hotel rooms. We were sneaking in a quick couples' tour of London before returning home.

"I think the two sisters needed the drama and trauma of their escapade to reunite at this deeper level," Kellie said. "I think that getting away from home and expanding your comfort zone causes you to see more clearly what matters most in your life."

"You're right," Martin and Roger said in unison. Both of them were looking affectionately at us, their adventuresome wives. The trip benefited all of us in appreciating our spouses more.

It's been two years since all this happened. We hear from Opal often, and it's almost always good news. She continually invites us to come visit again, and we might one of these days. But we've been pretty busy with some happy adventures of our own.

Kellie and LeeAnne have experienced stunning success with their interior-design business. Last month they were hired to redesign a pancake house in Orlando. Fifteen design companies entered bids, and K & L won. The theme they chose was a William Morris–inspired English cottage design, complete with a doormat that read "Go Away" and overly floppy white chef's hats. The owner thought the design was "original and brilliant."

I started volunteering at the children's hospital three days a week. I'm doing what makes me so happy I could burst. I sit beside ill children, and I read English classics to them. I take their frightened hearts and their waning imaginations and give them something to dream of. The dreams I instill in these children are not just dreams of pirate ships, street waifs, and nannies that can fly—although they have enjoyed all those stories. The dream I plant in them is a dream of heaven.

It all happened naturally the first time I read to a nine-year-old girl recovering from a car accident. I told her about my crush on Big Ben and how I at long last got my wish to see him face to face. She grinned when I recited my little poem to her.

Then I told her my truest dream: that one day I would see almighty God face to face because I had put my trust in Christ. His arms would always be open, and His face would always light up for any who came to Him.

Over the weeks and months that I returned to volunteer at the hospital, I repeated my story every time before reading from one of the classics. The nurses were thrilled with my visits. One of the mothers said her son told her I was an angel.

"What are you telling our son?" the mother asked me.

I looked her in the eye and said, "I'm telling him about two things of which I'm quite passionate, English literature and God, my heavenly Father."

In the two years I've been doing this, no one has complained or asked me to curtail my passion. Every time I show up at the hospital, I give myself permission to take a risk and tell a child about my growing love for God. And every time I step into that unknown chasm of untamed air, I watch my own fear fly away as I'm upheld by the everlasting arms.

So far, fourteen children have asked me to pray with them when they asked Christ to be the Lord of their young hearts. I smile my best smiles then, because I think of what it's going to be like one day when every knee bows and every tongue confesses that Jesus Christ is Lord.

We're just getting a head start here in the children's ward.

Reader's Guide

1. Liz and Kellie had lifelong dreams and wishes that came to fruition when they were in their fifties. What are your lifelong dreams? Do you have a childhood wish yet to come true? Are you willing to take a risk in order for your dream to unfold?

2. Instead of Stonehenge, the Tower Bridge, or the moors of Emily Brontë's *Wuthering Heights,* Liz's first view of England was of afternoon traffic in a modern city complete with billboards, asphalt, concrete buildings, and tinges of diesel fumes in the air. This first impression of England did not match her romantic expectations. Have you ever moved toward a dream only to be confronted with something ordinary? How did you respond?

3. Just as twins Opal and Rose finish each other's sentences, Liz and Kelly have their own understanding of each other, communicating with nonverbal gestures. Do you have someone in your life with whom you have such understanding? How might this relate to your relationship with God?

4. After leaving Olney, Liz and Kellie wound up in Oxford instead of London as they had planned. Sometimes the smallest life choices can take us to places we didn't intend to go. Have you ever experienced a significant detour in your life? What caused it, and what did you learn from it?

5. During their unplanned tour of Oxford, Liz and Kellie began to feel as if God had become their tour director, guiding them to significant places and sights. When have you felt God leading you from behind the scenes in your own life? To what significant places did He guide you? For what purpose?

6. Floating high above the Oxford countryside in a hot-air balloon, Liz and Kellie acknowledged they were having "an exceptional day," implying more than beautiful weather. Describe an exceptional day you've experienced. What events or sensations made it exceptional?

7. Kellie's playful humor helped Liz cope with the embarrassment of ripping her jeans before the hot-air balloon ride. Who or what cheers you up in uncomfortable situations? Do you allow yourself to laugh under such circumstances?

8. Liz became acutely aware of her own affluence while shopping at Harrods, so much that she suddenly felt spoiled. While enjoying tea at the Ritz, Kellie stated, "We are extravagantly, incredibly blessed. This is a rare abundance." How would you describe abundance in your own life? When you take time to count your blessings, do you ever feel spoiled? humbled?

9. Before the trip to England, Liz lived in a comfortable routine without many expectations of what God might do next in her life. Through the course of events in London, she realized how emotionally disconnected she was from God, and she saw how He had done more than they had expected in blessing their trip. Have you experienced emotional distance from God? What, if anything, helped you close the gap again?

10. Liz became separated from Kellie in the London underground. After initial feelings of panic, Liz felt peace and an assurance that God would lead her to find Kellie. However, it still took several hours for her to make her way back to the hotel where they would reunite. Have you ever felt so lost? When was the last time you felt the Lord's presence and protection?

11. Liz and Kellie supported and helped fulfill each other's dreams. How have your friends supported your dreams? In what ways have you shown support for theirs?

12. On the last day in London, Liz realized she had returned wholeheartedly to the Lord because He had given her a heart to recognize Him through the events of the trip. In what ways do you recognize God in your life? How do those things draw your heart toward Him?

Bonus Material for

Go Brit!

Hello, dear Sisterchick!

One of my greatest delights in writing the Sisterchicks novels has been the journeys I've taken around the world while researching the location of each book. (I know, what a writer's dream!) If I could take you with me on these adventures, oh what a time we would have! Since that's not possible, I thought you might enjoy seeing a few snapshots and hearing a few of the stories behind the story for *Sisterchicks Go Brit!*

TEATIME

No trip to England would be complete without a few proper teatimes. Our first was in Bedford, which just so happens to be where the tradition of British afternoon tea was instituted by Anna, the Duchess of Bedford. Our hosting party was a group of enthusiastic readers who call themselves the Blessed Chicks. Since our visit, two of these God-loving women have moved— one to New Zealand, one to the U.S.—yet they're staying connected through prayer and lots of e-mails. It's clear that women around the world love to gather not only to giggle but to lovingly support each other. We felt right at home.

A bit of silliness with the Blessed Chicks

Our most cozy teatime was in Olney at a quaint shop called Teapots. My editor, Julee, my British writer friend Marion Stroud, and I bent our heads close in calming conversation and did a little dreaming together. A lovely way to hush a busy day.

Teapots in Olney. Inside you'll find a darling collection
of old hats hung on the wall in the stairwell.

While in London, Julee, Marion, and I then connected with
Veronica Heley and Penny Culliford, two British novelists, and
indulged in a very posh high tea at the Ritz. Pinkies up!

Tea at the Ritz, from left to right: Robin, Penny, Marion,
Julee, and Veronica

OXFORD ADVENTURES

Our tour of Oxford was almost as wild and wacky as the account I fictionalized in the book. We loved the bookstores, the many chapels such as Exeter, and views of all the "dreaming spires." A highlight in this fabulous city was visiting Holy Trinity Church near the Kilns and sitting in the pew where C. S. Lewis sat every Sunday for decades. I loved trying to see what he saw and imagine what he imagined. And, yes, Tolkien's home did have lawn gnomes in the yard.

When we entered the chapel at Exeter, the Bible was open to Jeremiah and a student was practicing the organ in the balcony.
It was one of those moments when it felt as if the majesty of God was seeping through invisible walls and shining on us.

Yes, that's Ben in the background. Isn't he handsome?

LONDON SIGHTS

I love so many of the typical tourist sights in London that it was challenging to limit what was included in Kellie and Liz's adventure. Portobello Road is always at the top of my list along with Westminster Abbey and, of course, a long walk across Westminster Bridge at sunset to see Big Ben. Just like Liz, I think I've always had a little crush on Ben. His face lit up at twilight is unforgettable.

ON THE TRAIN TO WINDSOR CASTLE

Julee and I met Christelle on the way to Windsor in the same way that Kellie and Liz met Annette. The three of us chummed around the castle and shared a few giggles over tea and scones. Blessedly, Christelle's English far surpassed our French, and we were reminded once again that Sisterchicks are everywhere. Sometimes all it takes is a kind "hello" to start a friendship. Christelle and I still correspond. Not by e-mail. No. This woman who is young enough to be my daughter writes to me on fancy stationery with carefully penned sentences, and I respond in kind. This lingering souvenir of our day at the castle makes our small, across-the-ocean friendship that much more endearing.

On the castle grounds with Christelle at Windsor

I was trying to come up with a Beefeater expression to match
the one on my wooden friend. How did I do?

My Sisterchick Julee had a kinder, gentler approach
to making friends with the Beefeater.

A Few Tips on Some London Favorites

- Best Scones: The Orangery at Kensington Palace
- Best Time to Visit Portobello Road: Early! Shops open at 5:30 a.m. on weekends.
- Getting Around Town: Try it all—bus, taxi, underground, and your own happy feet.
- Churches: With such fabulous variety and unique history to each church, visit as many as you can. I love Sunday morning service at St. Paul's Cathedral and evening vespers at Westminster Abbey or at St. Martin-in-the-Fields.
- Outside of London: Take a bus to Oxford and include time to see the charming Cotswolds. Take a train to Windsor or Hampton Court and spend the day walking, gazing, and dreaming.

www.robingunn.com
www.sisterchicks.com

Shimmering Bits

FROM ROBIN'S NEST

*"You cast your net on the other side [of the boat],
and look at all the shimmering bits of glory
you're pulling in now!"*

—PENNY, *SISTERCHICKS ON THE LOOSE!*

When we reach heaven, my best friend, Donna, and I want to introduce you to a woman we met in Latvia. Her name is Marija, and to be honest, neither of us wanted to go to her house to see her. But, oh, what a moment of glory we would have missed!

Donna and I went to Latvia in 1993 to bring chocolate chips and cheer to a young missionary wife. I was invited to speak to the women at a church in the capital city, Riga. After an already full day, our interpreter asked if we would consider going to visit a woman who was ill.

I looked at Donna; she looked at me. We had spent the day sharing our hearts, teaching from the Bible, and standing for hours, listening through an interpreter to dozens of hurting women as they looked to us for any drop of encouragement. Since it now was after nine at night, I was ready to find a few nourishing morsels of food and fall into the nearest bed. Offering my weary self to all the germs of an ill person seemed like a bad idea.

"It's up to you," Donna said, giving me a bedraggled look.

Apparently it wasn't truly up to me, because even though my mind was saying, "Sorry, no," my mouth somehow translated those two simple words into, "Okay, we'll go." What is it the Bible says about the Spirit of God interceding for us? Does He transpose our intentions for us as well?

We were offered a ride to Marija's house so we wouldn't have to depend on the public tram. Unfortunately, the hospitality offered exceeded the maximum load capacity available. Like a troupe of circus clowns, we smushed seven bodies into a Soviet sedan built for four.

"You're squashing me," I murmured into the back of Donna's head. She was smaller and hence given the princess position on my lap.

"You're hogging all the legroom," she countered under her breath.

"Am not. Stop jiggling."

"I'm not jiggling. It's the road, or should I say, the ruts in the road?"

Our interpreter squeezed a peek at us from her two-to-a-front-seat position. "All is okay?"

I'd forgotten that anyone else in the car spoke English and could understand our squabbling. Donna and I have been known to have our feisty moments. We've found that exchanging dialogue as if we were childhood sibling rivals defuses tension. Our interpreter, however, didn't know that.

"All is okay?" she asked again. "We have only another ten minutes to drive."

"Ten minutes?" I groaned, feeling my legs going numb.

"This was your idea," Donna muttered.

I would have pinched her accessible backside, but my hand was wedged behind the door handle.

Our ten-minute ride turned into twenty minutes. I felt as if we were being kidnapped. The dark skies hurled javelins of lightning followed by roars of thunder. Apparently Donna and I weren't the only two elements having a spat that night.

The clown car came to an abrupt stop in front of a dilapidated manor that I felt I'd seen before—when I had toured a Hollywood studio and viewed a set for the original *Addams Family* show. Or was it *The Munsters*?

Big drops of rain pelted us as we performed a series of unattractive contortions to extract our bodies from the car. I opened my travel umbrella, but a gust of wind popped it inside out. Nothing about this moment felt good.

We dashed to the front door, where a flickering overhead light welcomed us. I held my breath. Not because I expected to be greeted by Cousin Itt, but because it smelled awful. Like dead cats. The woman who opened to our late-night knock wasn't Morticia, but Marija's full-time caregiver. She ushered us quietly into what had once been the dining room of this large house. In typical Communist fashion, the upstairs and downstairs had been converted into many cubicles of space with a separate family occupying each cubicle.

Tentatively approaching the corner, where a single lamp was lit, we came as close as we dared to the narrow bed where the diminished invalid sat, propped up by a pillow. Her white hair was clean and combed back from her glowing face. I hadn't expected Marija to be so astonishingly beautiful.

At first I wondered if the dim light on this elderly woman's pale skin gave her such a glow. Or did she have a fever? A contagious sort of fever that made her look rosy, vital, and yet oh so infectious?

She stretched out her right hand, eager to greet us, to touch us. Her fingers curled in, her wrist was bent. Yet she smiled radiantly. Donna and I hung back, waving our hellos rather than making contact with her. Then I noticed that Marija had no lumps under the covers where her legs should have been. Her left hand lay motionless at her side.

Marija wasn't sick. She had contracted polio forty years ago, when part of the remedy included amputation.

Donna and I were offered two of the three wobbly straight-backed chairs available. Marija began at once to roll out her grace-story for us. Our interpreter could barely keep up as Marija described her losses: a baby at birth, another child in his toddler years, and her husband soon after he was drafted into the Russian army. By the time she was twenty-two, Marija had lost almost everything. Then the polio came and took her legs.

The demure woman spoke softly, with her chin down, as she described how angry she had been with God and how deep the darkness that seemed to swallow her for several years. Then she asked God a question. Not a "why" question, but a "what" question. "What can I possibly do for You now? I am of no use."

And God answered her.

I looked at the others. They didn't blink at her statement. This woman said God answered her. He spoke to her. Was that why her countenance glowed? What does God say to such a small, broken woman on the other side of the world?

With clear, honest eyes, Marija spoke, and her answer was translated. "God told me He took my legs so I would not run around on this earth. Nearly anyone can do that. He asked me to do something different for Him. Something special. Something not everyone can do. He asked me to run every day between this earth and heaven and to carry up to Him the heart cries of His children. This is my job. My purpose. I run to heaven every day."

The room became very still. Donna and I sat with tears shimmering in our eyes, unashamed to let them fall without a sound onto our folded hands in our laps. I found it easy to believe that every time Marija stepped into those courts of heaven, she returned to earth with a bit of glory dust on her face. That was why she glowed.

Our interpreter went on to add that Marija used her crippled hand to write letters to encourage believers around the world. She wrote to Corrie ten Boom once, and Corrie, via an interpreter, wrote her back.

Marija's eyes twinkled at the name Corrie ten Boom. I had met Corrie in California, and that was why Marija wanted to meet me. I worked for a ministry organization that handled all of Corrie's correspondence during the year *The Hiding Place*, the movie about her life in a concentration camp during World War II, was released.

Marija pulled the crumpled letter from under her pillow and reached out her hand to show it to me. One of her most treasured possessions was this letter from Corrie, a woman who knew what it was like to be swallowed by darkness.

Oh, what a gift Donna and I would have missed if we hadn't been willing to "cast our nets on the other side," so to speak, of our schedule and energy to visit Marija. We're still feeding off the shimmering bits of glory pulled up during that exchange.

When it was time to go, Donna and I stood and went over to Marija to curl our arms around her. I pressed my cheek against hers and whispered a blessing, sealing it with a kiss on that rosy, glowing face. She drank it in and blessed me back, promising to pray for Donna and me every day.

Then one November morning, two years after we kissed Marija's face, she made her daily run to heaven, and this time Jesus told her she could stay.

*O*h, Marija, what a picture of grace your life was! You give all of us a new perspective on the struggles we face each day.

Nearly all of us have found ourselves in situations in which we felt like the pregnant woman who wishes she could skip that whole delivery thing. You know, no way out but the way we would prefer to avoid. None of us wants to suffer pain or loss of any kind. We don't ask for something like a physical disability or a lifelong battle with mental illness. But when life's overwhelming challenges come, the only road available is the one that goes right through the pain.

Have you been around someone who has been through some dark valleys? How did that person's experience change your perspective on your life circumstances?

With the blessings of Marija's daily trips to heaven on the wings of prayer, she glowed like an otherworldly saint. But when we see her losses and pain, her oh so normal bout with depression and anger, we know she is one of us.

Has there been a time when you found yourself feeling angry with God or others over your circumstances? For most of us, anger is an unavoidable place to travel through during tough times. While we may not be able to avoid visiting "anger," we certainly don't want to make it our permanent address!

In His kindness to us, the Lord says, "Go ahead and be angry. You do well to be angry—but don't use your anger as fuel for revenge. And don't stay angry. Don't go to bed angry. Don't give the Devil that kind of foothold in your life" (Ephesians 4:26–27).

When we choose to push beyond the anger, through the gate of surrender, we find the peace and joy that initially seemed impossible. Marija surrendered her anger to God, and she glowed. Well, guess what? So can we! This is how it happens: "Do everything without complaining or arguing, so that you may become blameless and pure, children of God without fault in a crooked and depraved generation, in which you shine like stars in the universe as you hold out the word of life" (Philippians 2:14–16, NIV).

So, go ahead—you glow, girl!

Whoa...it's getting shimmery bright in here! Glory!

TAKE A CLOSER LOOK

- Psalm 91:14–16. Hold on for dear life.
- Daniel 12:3. More shining and glowing.
- 2 Corinthians 1:8–12. A reason for hope for those in need.

A Peep or Two from You

_____

_____

_____

_____

_____

_____

_____

_____

_____

 Wisdom

"Consider it a sheer gift, friends,
when tests and challenges come at you
from all sides.
You know that under pressure, your faith-life is
forced into the open and shows its true colors.
So don't try to
get out of anything prematurely. Let it do its
work so you become mature and well-developed,
not deficient in any way."

James 1:2—4

QUOTABLE SISTERCHICKS

"Make sure that you let God's grace work
in your souls by accepting whatever
He gives you, and giving Him whatever
He takes from you. True holiness consists
in doing God's work with a smile."

MOTHER TERESA OF CALCUTTA

More SISTERCHICK®
Adventures by
Robin Jones Gunn

SISTERCHICKS ON THE LOOSE!

Zany antics abound when best friends Sharon and Penny take off on a midlife adventure to Finland, returning home with a new view of God and new zest for life.

SISTERCHICKS DO THE HULA!

It'll take more than an unexpected stowaway to keep two middle-aged Sisterchicks from reliving their college years with a little Waikiki wackiness—and learning to hula for the first time.

SISTERCHICKS IN SOMBREROS!

Two Canadian sisters embark on a journey to claim their inheritance—beachfront property in Mexico—not expecting so many bizarre, wacky problems! But there's nothing a little coconut cake can't cure!

SISTERCHICKS DOWN UNDER!

Kathleen meets Jill at the Chocolate Fish Café in New Zealand, and they instantly forge a friendship. Together they fall head over heels into a deeper sense of God's love.

SISTERCHICKS SAY OOH LA LA!

Painting toenails and making promises under the canopy of a princess bed seals a friendship for life! Fifty years of ups and downs find Lisa and Amy still Best Friends Forever…and off on an unforgettable Paris rendezvous!

SISTERCHICKS IN GONDOLAS!

When Jenna is invited to Venice for a week of cooking for a small retreat group, she knows just who to take along: her sister-in-law Sue. Sue actually knows how to cook (unlike Jenna)! Come join Jenna and Sue over boiling pots of pasta in this lilting gondola-paced adventure!

www.sisterchicks.com

THE GLENBROOKE SERIES

by Robin Jones Gunn

COME TO GLENBROOKE...

A QUIET PLACE WHERE SOULS ARE REFRESHED

SECRETS *Glenbrooke Series #1*

Beginning her new life in a small Oregon town, high school English teacher Jessica Morgan tries desperately to hide the details of her past.

WHISPERS *Glenbrooke Series #2*

Teri went to Maui hoping to start a relationship with one special man. But romance becomes much more complicated when she finds herself pursued by three.

ECHOES *Glenbrooke Series #3*

Lauren Phillips "connects" on the Internet with a man known only as "K.C." Is she willing to risk everything...including another broken heart?

SUNSETS *Glenbrooke Series #4*

Alissa loves her new job as a Pasadena travel agent. Will an abrupt meeting with a stranger in an espresso shop leave her feeling that all men are like the one she's been hurt by recently?

CLOUDS *Glenbrooke Series #5*

After Shelly Graham and her old boyfriend cross paths in Germany, both must face the truth about their feelings.

WATERFALLS *Glenbrooke Series #6*

Meri thinks she's finally met the man of her dreams...until she finds out he's movie star Jacob Wilde, promptly puts her foot in her mouth, and ruins everything.

WOODLANDS *Glenbrooke Series #7*

Leah Hudson has the gift of giving, but questions her own motives, and God's purposes, when she meets a man she prays will love her just for herself.

WILDFLOWERS *Glenbrooke Series #8*

Gena Ahrens has invested lots of time and money in renovating the Wallflower Restaurant. Now her heart needs the same attention.

Grace...IT BIDS ME FLY
AND GIVES ME Wings

A SISTERCHICKS DEVOTIONAL

TAKE FLIGHT!

ROBIN JONES GUNN
& CINDY HANNAN

For every Sisterchick seeking a fresh time with God, this devotional/ponder/prayer/excuse-to-gather-together book will send you soaring. Inside, you'll find a collection of insightful devotions, key Scripture verses, and wit 'n' whimsy wisdom for the journey, along with Sisterchickin' suggestions for further reading, space to pen a peep or two, and more!